LAST GIRL ALIVE

A CSI REILLY STEEL NOVEL

CASEY HILL

ALSO BY CASEY HILL

SERIAL

VICTIM

HIDDEN

THE WATCHED

QUANTICO

ONE LITTLE MISTAKE

PRETTY GUILTY SECRETS

THE PERFECT LIE

LAST GIRL ALIVE

Copyright © Casey Hill 2022

The right of Casey Hill to be identified as the Author of the Work has been asserted by her in accordance with the Copyright, Designs and Patents Act 1988.

All rights reserved. No part of this publication may be reproduced, stored in a retrieval system, or transmitted, in any form or by any means without the prior written permission of the author. You must not circulate this book in any format.

All characters in this publication are fictitious and any resemblance to real persons, living or dead is purely coincidental.

1

'Shush,' she whispered 'You know how he gets ...'

Cici's stomach ached with fear and her heart hammered beneath her ribcage as she wrapped an arm around her sister's shoulders and placed her other hand gently across her mouth.

All was still; the calm after the storm. The only sounds were the ticking of the old grandfather clock in the hallway, interspersed by low almost inaudible staggered sobs from the kitchen.

It was pitch dark where they were, but the sisters always felt safe in their cubbyhole beneath the stairs. The tight space and tapered ceiling was comforting.

Though three-year-old Emmy was growing impatient.

'Me hungry.'

'Mama said to wait till she called us. Here, take Blankie.' Cici handed over the ragged old muslin that she typically teased her sister about, but felt grateful for now.

She pulled Emmy closer, laying her tiny head on her lap. Watched her twirl a fair ringlet through her finger and simultaneously suck her thumb as she clutched the blanket.

Then she strained her ears once again — the sobbing seemed to have stopped. It felt to Cici like they had been hidden away for hours, yet the noise of smashing dishes and vibration of furniture tumbling over, still rang in her ears.

He had been kind lately. It was so long since he'd needed to punish anyone. And they had tried so hard not to make him mad.

A stray tear ran down her cheek and dropped onto her sister's hair.

Finally exhausted, Cici rested her head against the wall behind her and drifted off, praying that this time their mother had not been too severely punished.

Then she bolted upright. Had she slept for a second — or an hour?

The clock still ticked away in the hall, while Emmy's breathing was deep and regular as her sister lay sleeping on her lap.

She still couldn't tell if it was day or night, though the rumbling of her stomach at least told her it had been a long time since she'd eaten.

Gently, she eased her snoozing sister's head away so she could edge towards the cubbyhole doorway.

She knew that Mama had warned her to stay in here, yet something was wrong, something was ... different.

Cici crouched through the small door and stood up — a dart of pain shooting through her as she uncurled and fully straightened her body.

It was dark out; the only light coming from the partially ajar larder door. She stealthily pushed it open, heart in mouth as she tried to be quiet.

The harsh bright of the florescent lights caused her to raise her hand to her face as she tried to make sense of the scene.

She'd seen him face-down and passed out many times before after drinking that nasty water. But this time, a dark crimson pool surrounded his form and there was something ... a handle ... protruding from his back.

Cici felt no urge to run and check on him; on the contrary, she felt some of her fear subside.

Then hearing a noise from nearby, she turned quickly to look for her mother, but instead saw Emmy's eyes squinting in the light, as her baby blankie fell to the floor.

2

Sean Shaughnessy was not a man who scared easily.

He'd been swimming in the shark-infested waters of Dublin's criminal justice system for a long time, and represented some of the city's most prolific criminals. His allegiances had made him very wealthy and feared by his Law Society peers.

So the house alarm alert on his phone was just a nuisance, but likely nothing more than that. Robber scum knew to steer clear of his gaff if they valued their kneecaps. The advantage of friends in high (or low) places, depending on your perspective.

Course there was always a chance of some random junkie or blow-in operating in the area, but Sean knew a couple of phone calls would soon sort that kind of thing without having to deal with cops or insurance companies.

Nothing to worry about.

He pulled up to the gates of his house and pressed the mounted buzzer on the right-hand side pillar, before the electronic gates started to open.

The external beacon was flashing, but the noise was low; meaning the alarm had been going off for over thirty minutes before switching to quieter volume so as to avoid breaking sound pollution laws.

Sean stopped his Jaguar F-type between the pillars, blocking the sensor beam to stop the gates closing.

Better safe than sorry.

If some chancer happened to bolt from the house, better to give them an escape route than have them trapped like a rat in a corner.

Switching off the car engine, he glanced up at the front windows to check for any signs of life, but nothing.

Still, an inexplicable wave of anxiety crossed his mind before he shook it off and prepared to make a dash to the door to avoid getting wet in the rain.

Key in hand, Sean went to put it into the lock and reached for the front door handle.

As he did, a brief spark of light flashed across his eyes, the skin of his hand seemed to become at one with the handle, and his body was wracked with instant searing pain.

The scent of burning flesh and melting skin were the last sensory messages relayed through his nervous system; accompanying violet spasms so severe they caused several of his joints to dislocate, before finally Sean's heart stopped beating altogether. What skin remained melting on his fingers slid from the handle, and he slumped to the ground in a smouldering heap.

3

Detectives Chris Delaney and Pete Kennedy drove hurriedly along the bus lane, blue lights flashing and sirens blaring.

'Out of the way, gobshite,' Kennedy flattened his palm to the centre of the steering wheel, adding a car horn to the cacophony. 'Feck's sake, they could do with teaching some of these morons in the driving test how to respond to emergency vehicles ...' Glaring at the driver as he passed, he eventually manoeuvred the car onto the footpath.

Chris couldn't help but cringe upon seeing a hapless pensioner hunched over the steering wheel of the offending car.

'Poor old divil probably thought you were trying to pull him over for using the bus lane,' he said, steadying himself as the tyres bounced on dismounting the kerb. 'Next left should be us.'

He indicated to a tidily landscaped South Dublin

housing estate entrance; a large granite boulder with the name of the development engraved across the front.

A little way in, ambulance lights were already visible five or six doors up on the left hand side, and first responders walked sideways past a car partially blocking the entrance to the property that was their destination.

A uniform came to greet the two as they approached the house.

'Garda O'Rourke - you might remember we worked on the Staunton case out in Howth a couple of years back.'

'Ah, yes — how are things?' Chris expertly feigned recognition before moving swiftly on. 'What's the story here?'

O'Rourke grimaced. 'Messy one. You might have heard of the deceased - Sean Shaughnessy? Criminal lawyer for the rich and infamous.'

'Holy shit, Sean Shocks? They'll be wailing in the valley tonight so,' Kennedy said, referring to the drug crime stronghold on the Northside of the city known as The Valley, and where criminal defence lawyer Sean 'Shocks' Shaughnessy was something akin to a god.

The three men continued to talk as they walked toward the house, Chris zipping up his jacket to protect against the driving rain.

'To be honest, we thought it was a domestic thing when it was called in by some fella delivering junk mail ...' O'Rourke moved though the gateway blocked by a brand new Jaguar, and the detectives followed; Kennedy's amble girth necessitating a squeeze up against the soaking wet chassis.

'Wouldn't it be more in your line to get this thing out of the bloody way?' he grunted as he (only just) cleared the gap between car and pillar.

'It's locked. Keys are on the victim, but to be honest nobody is inclined to go searching for them...' O'Rourke stood to the side and indicated a crumpled heap outside the front entrance to the house.

Chris's nose wrinkled and he instinctively put a hand to his mouth as he got closer. Even in this wind it was still possible to pick up the stench of burnt flesh.

And coming closer, it became pretty obvious why nobody wanted to seek out Sean Shaughnessy's car keys.

'Good Jaysus...' Kennedy muttered to nobody in particular.

It looked as though a single key had somehow become fused with the victim's right hand while others in the bunch had melted into his palm.

The lawyer's body was face down in front of the door, legs twisted beneath him at impossible angles. It was a horrific spectacle and a new one for Chris, who at this stage thought he'd seen everything.

'You said you thought a domestic accident at first?' he looked dubiously at O'Rourke.

The officer nodded. 'Power surge or something. First thing we did was go around the back to look for the meter box — see if it had tripped out maybe.' O'Rourke led them back towards the rear of the house. 'That's when we saw this.'

A glass panel in the back door was smashed and the door itself stood wide open, while a mixture of muddy footprints and windswept rainwater coated the floor beneath.

Through the doorway, they could see back through the house and Chris spied an electric cable leading from a nearby socket to the front door; the wire crudely attached to the metal handle with duct tape.

For some reason the set-up put him in mind of that old Christmas movie, *Home Alone.*

Except it obviously wasn't the Sticky Bandits they were dealing with here.

'GFU notified?' Kennedy asked, referring to the forensic unit.

O' Rourke nodded. 'Yeah, Steel's on her way.'

'She's back on the job ... already?' Surprise evident in his partner's voice, he looked at Chris as if he had all the answers.

He nodded, unwilling to get into anything in front of the other officer. 'Apparently so.'

The truth was, Chris hadn't been a hundred percent sure she would come back to work so soon — the last time they'd spoken she'd been pretty adamant about it, but still ...

'Well, that car out front's going to cause an ongoing access issue. We'll have to move it somehow,' he pointed out, shuddering a little as he thought again about those keys encrusted with melted human flesh.

'Has anybody been inside the house yet?' Kennedy asked.

'We checked it out — all clear and nothing live - power-wise, I mean. Also flipped the mains switch; everything on the board was sealed down with duct tape to prevent any tripping out. Obviously, someone wanted to make sure he was hit with a full-on mains jolt.'

'Get someone back there to look for a spare car key — the usual places, drawers hooks, or whathave-you. But don't go too mad rooting around either — we don't want to mess up forensics.'

'And if we can't find one?'

'Make a call to Traffic, get them to send a transporter to lift it out or something,' Chris suggested.

Multiple people tramping through a crime scene was an obvious GFU bugbear that everyone was keen to avoid.

But Chris couldn't help but wonder if Reilly would be as energised about this stuff as normal — since lately, that famous 'Steel' edge had been blunted.

4
___

You can do this. Nothing's different. Just get your head back in game.

Reilly kept repeating the mantra, as inside the Garda Forensic Unit van, she went through the motions of putting coveralls over her clothing and readying herself for the first day back on the job.

She tried to click her brain in gear to initiate a broad-stroke sweep of her first crime scene in weeks.

Nothing was different. But everything had changed.

Outside the house, heavy gusts of wind swept the rain in sideways, but despite the air movement, the unmistakeable stench of burning skin assaulted her senses and the odour of charred flesh and excrement penetrated her face mask.

'Better get the tent up first?' her forensic tech

colleague Lucy suggested from beside her, startling her out of her reverie. 'With the weather and all ...'

She struggled to shake out the brain fog. 'Sure. Of course.'

As Gary, the other member of the team duly brought up the rear with the forensics tent, Reilly took a moment to look around, before resolutely ignoring the victim for the moment and heading for a side gate leading to the back of the house.

First things first.

'Good to have you back, pet,' Kennedy called out; his voice gentle as he came up behind her and she noted that for once, the older detective hadn't greeted her as Goldilocks.

And so it begins ...

'Oh hey,' she replied her voice bright. 'I'd love to say it's great to *be* back, but you know...' she smiled tightly, indicating the ghoulish scene at the front door and then upwards at the rain and wind, which seemed to be getting worse.

Chris followed his partner and briskly greeted the GFU crew before approaching her, his face expressionless.

'Straight back in at the deep end, eh?' he joked lightly, as the wind funnelled sheets of rain down the side passage. 'It's more sheltered back here,' he added leading her round to the rear of the property where a sodden uniform stood on sentry duty.

'So, what have we got?' Eager to avoid any small

talk, Reilly looked inside the damaged back door; her gaze automatically scanning the area beneath the broken glass pane.

Chris, poised to take her lead, also launched straight into professional mode.

'Apparent point of entry through the glass panel, as per footprints through the kitchen to the hallway. First responder went in to check if anybody else was inside, and to ascertain the power supply situation,' he explained, indicating the electricity wires attached to the door handle.

'Trip switches were jammed with duct tape, so it was the main fuse that blew in the end. Poor divil took a right jolt.' Kennedy added, trying to shelter as much of his large frame as possible from the elements under the roofline. 'Ironic really.'

'How so?' Reilly queried.

'His name is Sean Shaughnessy - lawyer to the rich and infamous. Didn't know him personally, but by all accounts he was a smug git whose trade involved keeping dealer scumbags out of jail too. Goes by the nickname 'Shocks' because he has a tendency for theatrics in the courtroom.'

'Possibly gangland related then. Retribution from a rival crew who took the nickname a bit too literally?'

Chris shrugged. 'Not so sure - this guy was pretty much everyone's friend, except ours obviously. He didn't play sides. All the bigger players in the city would want - or more to the point - *need* him alive and on form.'

'Plus whoever set this up was either very brave or completely thick,' Kennedy pointed out. 'When the house alarm went off, they couldn't have known the response time. So to break the glass, rig the door and fuse board and just calmly walk off after, showed balls of steel. Bit like yourself,' he added jokingly and Reilly couldn't help but raise a smile at his attempt to lighten the situation for her benefit.

Typical...

'We were just about to question the young lad who found Shaughnessy in a heap like that at the door,' Chris told her. 'He's pretty shook up as you can imagine.' Then he winced at his own unintentional pun.

'Sure. We're pretty much all set here, so go ahead. I'll let you know if anything jumps out.'

Once again, Kennedy patted her on the shoulder, while Chris looked on awkwardly.

Strange, but she had automatically assumed that it would be the older detective who'd be fumbling his words, unsure what to say, but instead it was Chris - the one who knew her at her best (and worst) who seemed awkward about her being back in the field so soon.

But they'd already discussed this, and as far as she was concerned it was the preferred option.

She needed this.

Now she gave him a curt nod. 'Catch you later.'

Reilly breathed deeply, bracing herself as she pulled the coverall hood over her head, and stepped back into the only part of her life that had ever made sense.

5

Lucy reappeared from behind, carrying the kit bags. 'Where do you want to set up inside?'

'Maybe over in the corner beside the fridge,' Reilly replied to her colleague, her eyes following the trail of dirty footprints from the back door all the way through the hallway.

Lucy duly set the equipment down safely, before taking out a camera with a wide angled lens.

'Is the tent set up out front?' Reilly asked.

'Yep. Gary just needs to weight it down a bit, so it doesn't all take off with this wind.'

'Let's do a preliminary sweep here first before we head out.'

While Reilly walked the grid, Lucy began taking iSPI footage of the area, starting with the damaged back door, before working her way methodically through the kitchen, ensuring the 3D imaging software program would be able to recreate the scene back in the lab.

'Looks like a lot of fresh mud in here, so likely the perp came over the wall and through the shrubbery. Better take some tread impressions from outside, before the weather ruins everything.'

'Good idea.' Reilly crouched down to examine the best-preserved footprint inside the property. It was far enough from the back door that it had just the right amount of mud and moisture to leave a decent tread imprint. Luckily, they could easily differentiate any secondary tread from the first responders. The outline of standard issue police brogues was markedly different to the intruder's heavily textured trainer-style print.

She rose to her feet. 'What size shoe do you reckon?'

Lucy made a face. 'Not sure, but at first glance seems small - no more than a men's seven or eight?'

'That's what I thought; there's a couple more over there that are a little too faint for an impression lift, but maybe better suited for iSpi.'

'I'm on it.'

Satisfied that Lucy had everything under control in the kitchen area, Reilly made her way through into the hallway, her gaze scouring the ground as she went.

As she reached the front door, her gaze was drawn to the rigged door handle. Electrical wire had been wound around it a dozen or so times before trailing off to a nearby socket. Given the short timeline between the intruder alarm going off, and the time it would take to get things set up, she could only assume that the perp had brought the cable.

Which meant that their doer had planned ahead. Never a good thing from a forensic point of view.

She combed the area again a few times, before being drawn towards the fuse board. Duct tape had been applied unsparingly to ensure the trips were locked in position. The person they were looking for had absolutely thought this through and like Kennedy pointed out, determined to ensure that the unsuspecting victim received the maximum amount of volts, creating unfathomable pain and bodily trauma.

Sean Shocks...

Reilly shuddered, readying herself to see the results of all that, as she headed back outside to examine the corpse.

She approached the newly-erected forensic tent at the front door, and used both hands to separate the door flaps allowing entry. The other GFU crew member Gary, had also needed to set up a lighting rig, given the absence of sufficient natural light with the inclement weather - as well as weight down the canvas.

As she entered the enclosed space, now empty apart from its recently deceased occupant, her nose twitched. Smells were stronger and more apparent once the wind had less influence, and she couldn't escape that the scent of freshly-seared flesh put her in mind of Fourth of July summer cookouts back home in California. A grisly comparison considering.

She placed her kitbag on the ground and decided to remove her mask altogether, placing it high on her head.

A few murder by electrocution cases she'd worked on in the past involved electrical devices, accidentally or otherwise, being placed in a body of water. This one was very different, in that a strong voltage current had been conducted directly through flesh and blood.

And the results were ... not pretty.

The corpse lay in almost yoga-like stance - arms stretched out where the melted skin on one hand had eventually come free of the door handle, and the other had followed. The front door key remained in the lock while the rest were fused to the victim's hand, again tearing flesh off his palm as he'd crumpled to the ground.

The burn wounds on each hand were completely different colours; the left scorched black and brownish, while the wounds on the right; the hand in which he'd been holding the door key, were more yellow in appearance.

Reilly quickly surmised this differentiation as caused by various metal types on the keys and the door handle, which would have alternating burn properties.

She moved in for a closer look at the bunch of

keys. The fact that it was raining would have of course caused the victim's clothing to be wet, and therefore more conductive.

But this wasn't really enough to explain the extent and duration of the guy's electrocution. Generally, a fuse trip prevented the kind of huge surge that had obviously happened here.

Some electrical shocks were enough to jolt a person backwards and out of further danger, but if the current was high enough, it was often nigh on impossible to let go of an electrified object.

This poor victim's right hand had been twisted, burned and blistered to the point where metal had fused with flesh. Parts of the skin had also been burned off to reveal a network of tendons and delicate metatarsals.

Reilly also noted the faster onset of rigor mortis - common to electrical conduction - and which the M.E. would no doubt take into account when estimating time of death.

She stood up then and walked around to study the victim's face, noting the manner in which he had eventually slid into the position he was in now, that yoga-like 'child pose' - though the dislocation of one of his shoulders and both knees made his limbs look impossibly angled.

She also noted the inside left ankle area where the man's trouser ends had been burnt away to reveal naked bone, muscle and singed tendons, occurring while the current had flared and earthed itself through his foot.

Reilly hoped for Sean Shaughnessy's sake that his nervous system's capacity to relay pain messages to the brain had also quickly shut down given the force of the jolt.

His head was turned to the left, his visage pale but unmarked. Again as typical following electrical damage, the whites of both eyes were congested with blood and his pupils fully dilated.

Examining closer, Reilly took a few more camera shots and noticed his jaw also seemed somewhat misaligned on the opposite side to the one she was closest to. Perhaps dislocated when he slumped down and away from the handle, or by the electrical current itself?

Again, to be determined by the M.E.

Then Reilly set the device down and took out several numbered yellow markers.

Standing back, she visually scanned the area immediately surrounding the body, before starting to place photo markers at various places or objects of forensic interest: the victim's wallet, a discarded green apple that he must have been eating at the time, plus his phone on the ground nearby.

'How's it going in here?' Gary popped his head inside the tent.

'Almost done. Just about to do a quick roll before the M.E. arrives,' she replied, lint roller already in hand as she prepared to roll the victim's clothing for any further trace, despite the fact that there would be an inevitable level of contamination from weather exposure. 'You?'

'Getting through it.'

For once, Gary didn't follow up with any of his trademark smart-ass quips. Great. Now he was tiptoeing around her too.

It was her first day back after an admittedly short hiatus, but everyone seemed to be acting as if she'd been gone for a year.

And yet again, Reilly found herself feeling like she had something to prove.

6

'Deane, isn't it?' Chris asked, slipping into the driver's seat of the squad car, while his partner finished briefing the officer babysitting the witness who'd discovered Sean Shaughnessy's body. 'Just need to ask you a few questions before we get someone to drop you home.'

'Umm I already told the other Garda everything I know, but yeah ... OK,' he stuttered and Chris felt sorry for the kid, who looked to be about seventeen. Deane Kearney's Adam's apple bobbed and his expression was pale as he sat restlessly in the backseat of the squad car.

'Can you give us another rundown of events this morning?' he asked, without further preamble as Kennedy joined them.

'Well I...I was delivering leaflets first thing, and was nearly finished up in this estate which was my last before heading in for college.' The kid paused and looked out through the rain-soaked window. 'A lot of these gaffs have postboxes on the gates or pillars which speeds things up, even more so around here because a lot have those no junk mail stickers. Many of the other lads stick the leaflets in regardless, but I don't 'cos I know it only pisses people off,' he babbled nervously. 'Anyway, I saw the Jag parked in the gate there.' He motioned back toward the house. 'I noticed it because ... well it sounds stupid I know ... but if I ever win the Lotto, one of those new model F-Types is the first thing I'd buy.'

'I hear you,' Chris nodded, trying to establish a rapport.

'Even though it was pissing rain and I was pretty soaked, I decided to drop a leaflet to the front door so I could get a good look at the car from the front.' Deane took a sip from the almost empty coffee cup he'd been drinking. 'I'm kinda sorry I did now.' He gulped. 'At first, I thought it was a pile of clothes on the step. But I couldn't figure out why there was smoke coming off it ... till I got closer. That's when I got the smell and then I saw his hand....' He grimaced and his voice trailed off.

'Do you remember what time that was?' Kennedy prompted.

Deane thought for a moment and then straightened up for better access to his jeans pocket, before pulling out his phone.

'I rang 999 straight away and that call was at ... 11:47, so literally sixty seconds before.'

"That's helpful Deane, cheers. Anything else you noticed? Was the house alarm ringing at that point?'

He frowned. 'I don't think there was any alarm going. Not that I remember anyway.' He ran his fingers through his still-damp hair, his eyeballs shifting as he struggled to remember. 'I think it might have been ... beeping a bit, but it definitely wasn't ringing out loud full blast - I'm sure I'd have remembered that.'

Chris took a note of this. The first responders had also said the quieter secondary alarm was ringing when they arrived.

According to noise pollution directives, residential house alarms could by law ring externally for fifteen minutes only, before switching to a quieter setting. He made a mental note to have the alarm company build a timeline from the initial alarm trip to when Sean Shaughnessy was discovered.

'Grand, thanks. What did you do after you called emergency services?' Kennedy asked him.

'I didn't know what to do to be honest. I'm not squeamish, my Dad's a butcher, but I could see his arms and legs turned at that weird angle ... and the smell.' The kid shook his head. 'I knew he was gone - dead I mean. There was nothing else I could do to help. I went next door and rang the neighbours' bell, but I think your man must have thought I was a junkie or something when he came out 'cos I was pretty frantic.'

'The neighbour in number 25 - the house with

the red door on the left?' Chris clarified as he continued to make notes.

'Yeah, an older guy. Fair play - he came out and had a look, then rang the local station straight away too. His wife saw I was a bit shook, so she brought me in and sat me down with a cuppa while we waited for the cops ... I mean you guys, to arrive.'

'All right Deane, thanks for the moment. We have your details in case we need to follow up on anything, and I'll also give you my card if you remember something else about this morning - anything at all, no matter how unimportant, OK?'

He gulped again. 'OK.'

Immediately after, the detectives proceeded to interview some of the neighbours, including those at No. 25, who corroborated Deane's story and didn't appear terribly distressed that their infamous next neighbour was no longer of this world.

'I'm sorry for what happened to him but the same fella is no great loss,' the wife told them, scowling. 'Wouldn't give you the time of day.'

'She means that as neighbours go, Sean Shaughnessy pretty much kept to himself,' her husband added quickly, for fear they'd be labelled suspects, or worse, targets of any nefarious 'associates'. Though Chris had no immediate concerns on either score. 'Didn't put in or out with us or anyone else, nor go to any neighbourhood watch meetings or the like. Got the sense he had his own version of that, if you know what I mean.'

Chris did, and while it was evident that this couple was both aware and appalled that their next-door neighbour had links to some of the most notorious figures in organised crime, it was also clear that they weren't about to lose any sleep over his demise.

The remainder of his and Kennedy's neighbourhood door-to-door proved for the most part fruitless; the inclement weather had kept the majority of nearby residents inside, which pretty much meant that nobody had seen or heard anything unusual.

The ringing of the house alarm had also been attributed to the bad weather, and in any case the odd rogue alarm was the norm in a suburban housing estate.

The detectives eventually made their back to the house to see how the GFU team was doing. Given the victim's profile, some press reporters and TV cameras had appeared behind the police cordon, and the various journalists called out to them as they re-entered Sean Shaughnessy's property.

A TV news crew was setting up outside a house on the other side, and Chris knew that the evening reports would feature the obligatory 'shocked' local talking about how this was 'such a quiet and safe area, and nothing like that ever happened around here.'

He wondered if people truly believed that their own home patch was safe and quiet, or if they simply had a distorted view of reality to make themselves feel better. Chris knew from experience that quiet areas where 'nothing bad ever happened' didn't exist anymore.

While the rain had since eased a little, the wind still whipped at the canvas of the forensic tent sheltering the corpse and primary crime scene.

Out back, the detectives acknowledged a damp and frustrated-looking Gary on the lawn. The GFU tech had several sodden grass patches cordoned off and covered as he attempted to take tread impressions in the soft ground.

As they approached the back entrance to the house they saw Reilly and Lucy in the hallway deep in conversation whilst examining the contents of an evidence bag.

'Knock, knock,' Kennedy called out.

Reilly motioned with her index finger to let the detectives know she'd be with them shortly and finishing her exchange with Lucy, she joined them at the back door.

'How's everything going? We've a few on the way to Shaughnessy's ex wife's house to break the bad news, assuming she hasn't already heard.'

'Could be worse, could be his current wife,' Kennedy added wryly.

'I was actually thinking this place had a very bachelor feel, very few personal effects and definitely not much of a female influence.'

'Seems he lived alone here, despite a reputation of being a bit of a ladies' man. He and the wife separated a couple of years ago,' Chris told her. 'Divorce came through late last year. Not sure of his current relationship status, but we'll be heading to his office to question work colleagues,' he added, feeling slightly uncomfortable talking shop with her now. As if nothing at all had changed. 'Anything so far yourself?'

'Other than somebody went to a lot of trouble to put this together. They were either very cool or they knew the lay of the land.'

'How do you mean?' Kennedy asked.

'Well, for starters they seemed unperturbed by the alarm activation. Surely they must have been worried about somebody responding to it, police or even neighbours with a key...'

'Alarm was just a noise maker, no monitoring service apparently,' the big man told her. 'One of the first responders was already in touch with the home security company. They said it was an SMS alert set-up and the only number on file was Shaughnessy's mobile.'

'And no phone in the car, so I'm guessing the device was on his person,' Chris pointed out, with a grimace. 'Meaning any information on there is probably also fried to bejaysus.'

7

'Your turn to feed the pigs, I did it yesterday,' Cici cried out, as her sister passed by the pig pen, and instead disappeared into the barn towards her favourite animals.

The two girls sported rosy cheeks, as a cold gale swept through from a northerly direction funnelled by the valley walls. The bitter wind rattled the roof of the barn and the other animal shelters around the courtyard.

Inside, the barn was set out in sheep pens; a few containing ewes about to deliver the first of the spring lambs.

Emmy, who adored the animals was eager to see if any new youngsters had arrived.

Cici on the other hand, had long since distanced herself. When she herself was much younger, she had petted the lambs and like Emmy now, had once given them nicknames too.

But that was before she understood their purpose.

'Look, Mrs Snuffle's going to have her baby!' Emmy cried out with delight when she joined her inside.

'I told you stop giving them names,' Cici warned. 'It'll only make it harder.'

'Mrs Snuffle won't be dinner, silly - her job is just to have babies and we eat *those*,' her seven year old sister corrected without hesitation or emotion, before climbing into the pen and trotting over to the ewe. 'Mrs Snuffle, you're not dinner, are you?'

As the girls watched, the expectant sheep stood motionless while a membrane-and-mucus-covered newborn struggled out.

Emmy who at that tender age already had the confidence of an adult farmer, went behind Mrs Snuffle and gently applied pressure until the slimy lamb slid onto the straw covered ground.

'Is it OK?'

'Not sure, doesn't seem to be breathing,' Emmy frowned, pulling membrane away from the lamb's mouth and nose. She rose to her feet, holding the youngster's hind-legs and started to spin around in a circle, twirling the animal along with her.

Then laughed as some mucus flew off and hit Cici in the face, causing her to cry out in disgust. 'Ugh. You did that on purpose!'

Emmy put the lamb down, going into convulsions of laughter as her big sister frantically wiped her face and spat on the ground.

The ewe began to lick at the lamb as it took its first breath and instinctively shook its head to clear itself.

Emmy was still doubled over in laughter.

Until their mother appeared in the courtyard, and then the surrounding squeals from the adjoining pig pen were so high-pitched that the two girls had to hold their hands over their ears; the sound of terror and fear bouncing hollowly around.

A sharp blade in her hand, Lina gestured to the girls to follow her over to the pigs; knowing her words would be ineffective against the screaming.

Inside the other building, she held out the blade; sharp end facing inwards to allow the recipient to safely grasp the handle.

The same one that ...

Cici's face was deathly pale as she stared at the knife, horrified. Though her sister barely let a second pass before stepping forward to take it.

Then grabbing a nearby piglet, Emmy bent down and ran the sharp blade across its neck in a swift, sideways movement that immediately changed the atmosphere.

Almost like the flick of a switch.

Calm and quiet now; the only sound in the barn was the soft drip of blood landing on dirty straw.

When Cici was younger, Papa had tried to

explain to her that it was OK to feel sad, but to remember that this was simply 'all part of the circle of life.'

After that her enjoyment of *The Lion King* storybook was never the same. She felt so jealous of other kids - *normal* kids' - fairytale version of that notion. One that didn't include the bloodcurdling screams of a soon-to-be-slaughtered animal, and its mother.

'They are not *normal* kids though,' Mama argued, when Cici had shared her misgivings about killing the animals. 'They are doomed children who have no sense of reality, living their lives in a virtual world that has been created purely to distract and subjugate them. I know it's hard sometimes, but you must understand; when the tide turns on this world and true reality dawns, you two will have the skills to survive whereas they will not.'

Mama always had a way of making Cici feel better.

The way Papa told stories of the outside world often left her scared - terrified even - whereas Mama had a way of explaining things that made her feel lucky not to be 'normal.'

'You can't let your sister take responsibility for this stuff all the time,' her mother said now, putting a hand on Cici's shoulder. 'You're the older one, remember.'

'It's OK, I don't mind,' Emmy smiled, eyes gleaming as she wiped blood from the blade with a handful of straw. 'I know she's not as brave as me.' Then her sister glanced dispassionately back down at the piglet. 'Dinner is served.'

8

Later that evening, laden down with a couple of Donnybrook Fair's finest ready-meals he'd picked up on the way, Chris knocked on Reilly's front door.

While he hoped that her first week back wouldn't be quite so ... intense and that she could've done with a couple of easier stints in the lab for a bit; in this business, a more straightforward transition was almost too much to ask for.

Still, he was pleased to note that she'd seemed pretty much back to herself earlier at Shaughnessy's house, and laser-focused on the task in hand as always.

The utmost professional.

But now he wanted to be sure that her GFU game face wasn't just that - a facade.

'Hey.' She seemed surprised to see him and her

gaze moved to the paper bag he was carrying. 'Kinda late for a house visit ...'

Reilly stood back from the doorway to let him in, and Chris immediately knew by her hollowed-out eyes and tired demeanour that today had indeed taken a lot more of out her than she'd anticipated.

Granted, they were both used to long days spent out in the field or at the office pouring over case files and what-have-you, but this was different.

'I know, but I'm guessing you haven't had dinner, yet?' Bad enough that she pretty much always forgot to eat when in the middle of an investigation, but over the last while he knew she wouldn't have remembered to eat food at all if Chris hadn't insisted on it.

And for the most part, prepared it for her.

In the kitchen, he popped the pasta trays into the microwave and took out some plates and cutlery, chatting easily as he went.

'Helluva day wasn't it? Straight back in at the deep end but what else is new. Good thing the rain stopped finally - I nearly needed a change of - '

'Chris, you can't keep doing this. I told you, I'm OK.'

'Doing what? I was getting grub anyway; might as well save you having to think about it after a long day.'

'I have eaten actually.'

'Great, more for me, so.' Though he was a little thrown that she'd already sorted something. But hey, that was a good sign too. 'You love this carbonara though, so I'll do a small plate for you anyway.'

She exhaled. 'Honestly, I'm fine - I won't be joining you. Actually, if you don't mind, I'd rather just get an early night.'

He looked directly at her for the first time all day, noticing the change in her voice and body language. She was detached ... cold almost.

OK, so maybe today hadn't been so great after all.

'Hey ...' Coming out from behind the kitchen counter, he moved to take one of her hands in his, but she deftly moved away.

'Sorry, I know you mean well, but I can't ... I actually need some time alone right now.'

He knew he shouldn't take it personally but still, the words stung.

After all the time they'd spent together over the last while - Chris practically living here, taking care of her, keeping a careful watch over her as she slept (or didn't), talking everything through.

Being there for Reilly when she needed someone to lean on after an unexpected issue with the pregnancy that was out of the blue and as yet, inexplicable.

Never in a million years would Chris be able to understand how it must feel for a woman to lose a baby so late in term, nor how harrowing it must be to have to deliver a non-viable foetus anyway.

Shortly after her most recent ultrasound which revealed the tragic news, Chris had driven Reilly to the hospital and stayed in the waiting room until she returned from the delivery suite, typically stoic but he guessed, numbed with shock in more ways than one - and had scarcely left her side since.

Most days she was pragmatic, insisting that it was all for the best and that she was never cut out to be a mother anyway. On others she was wracked with guilt, adamant that it was her own fault for essential denying the pregnancy for so long, to the point of putting herself and the baby in danger while on the job.

The one emotion she didn't seem to allow was grief. Almost as if she didn't deserve it.

And while Chris had gently pointed out that while a twenty-three week old foetus was in the eyes of the law considered incompatible with life, and thus technically a miscarriage as opposed to a stillbirth, that didn't mean that she shouldn't mourn the baby's demise, or worse, play it down.

But typically, Reilly seemed to find this technical element almost easier to process, and so he went along with that, happy to support her in every way he could in the aftermath of her loss, regardless of how she preferred to frame it.

He understood the emotional fallout of such a deeply personal, almost silent tragedy was bound to be especially complex for every parent - not least for one who hadn't quite yet come to terms with the prospect of having a child, let alone losing one.

And Reilly's thought process in general was nothing if not complex.

Though Chris certainly hadn't expected her to want to get back on the job so soon. Pretty much immediately after the requisite birth recovery time suggested by the hospital, Reilly was adamant that a prompt return to the lab was for the best - that it would give her something to focus on.

As close as they'd become over the last few weeks in particular, and how much she'd let him in or allowed herself to lean on him, Chris still understood how highly she valued her independence and how staunchly-prized was her work ethic. So he didn't argue or try to persuade her otherwise.

Still, that didn't mean he was happy to let her fend for herself just yet.

Looking at her now though; dark circles under her eyes and a haunted expression on her face as she stood facing him in her kitchen, he felt that perhaps he should have suggested she take a little more time. But of course it wasn't his place to suggest anything.

As she was clearly now reminding him.

'Of course,' he said, putting his hands in his jeans pockets. 'I just wanted to be sure you were OK after today.'

'I'm fine. You need to stop treating me with kid gloves, Chris. I won't break.'

'I know that, of course I do. But today wasn't exactly your run of the mill situation either.'

'Nothing ever is though, is it? You know that as

well as I do. But you're right about one thing - it was a long day. And I need an early night. I know that once everything truly kicks off on this thing and we start analysing, my brain will be going a mile a minute, so I just don't have time for ...'

He frowned. 'For what? A chilled-out chat over dinner with a friend? I know how these things work too, remember? Better than most.' He went to take the pasta out of the microwave, but put one steaming carton back into the bag. 'But yeah, you're right. Important to catch up on sleep. I'll get out of your hair and leave you to it.'

She sighed. 'I didn't mean you should leave right away. I was just saying...'

He knew he was being petulant and selfish too, but he couldn't help it. She was putting up those old defences and pushing him away.

Again.

And while Chris's rational side understood why she was doing it, his ego was winning and his pride crushed. Just when after all this time, they were getting somewhere. Moving forward, little by little with whatever this was.

Or so he thought.

'No it's fine. I get the message,' he said, sweeping everything back up and heading for the door. 'I'll leave you alone.'

9

The following morning, Reilly was heading for the GFU office bright and early, keen to get started on cataloguing yesterday's haul, when her phone rang.

After a brief conversation, she hung up and quickened her pace towards the lab. As she walked through the door she spied her colleagues chatting together at one of the workstations.

The team was such a well-oiled machine now; so used to working together in perfect harmony that she guessed they didn't especially miss her recent absence.

Even at the crime scene yesterday, she didn't need to direct or suggest anything; Gary and Lucy knew exactly what to do - had all the bases automatically covered.

Were those two still a couple? She couldn't be

sure. To be fair, they were very good at keeping their personal lives separate from professional.

And she herself needed to do the same.

'Morning,' they both greeted in unison.

'Not sure how good it's going to be. Seems we have another callout already.'

Reilly relayed the information she'd just been given.

A woman out walking her dog had stumbled upon a body just off the main trail of a popular Wicklow walking spot near the city border. The same area was the location of a current ongoing missing person search after a Dublin journalist was last seen in the same environs.

'Lucy, probably better you stay here and get ahead of everything from yesterday. Gary, come with me. Need to spread ourselves out on everything now, and I want to get down there for a preliminary sweep before the M.E. gets there.'

Her head swirled. Her first week back and already they were being snowed under.

She was relieved that one decision had been taken out of her hands though; the autopsy of that electrocuted defence lawyer was scheduled to take place later, and now she would be otherwise engaged.

While Reilly always made it her business to attend these things, the sight of a freshly carved up body on a mortuary slab would be a bridge too far just now…

. . .

SHE SAT in the passenger seat of the GFU van with Gary driving as they crossed the Wicklow/Dublin border and then left the motorway, heading into the mountains.

While Reilly had been up in these parts many times on hiking trails and on one memorable kidnapping case a while back, it was a huge area and mostly remote. Which is why she was happy to let the satnav direct them straight to where the emergency services were already located.

The location was a good way off-road along the side of a moderate hiking trail, with the closest vehicle access point some twelve hundred meters away.

'No Batman and Robin today,' Gary mused out loud.

'Sorry, what...?' She was lost in her own thoughts.

'This is a good way off their patch isn't it?'

'Yeah, someone more local I guess.' This time, she was relieved not to have to see or deal with Chris - after last night especially. She hadn't intended to be so dismissive, or offend him like she clearly had, but she needed to get back on her own two feet.

She hadn't been lying to him either; yesterday had been exhausting in more ways than one. She was just a little out of practice, that's all. And having so much to contend with just now was a blessing in disguise really. Exhaustion helped you sleep at night.

Looking up the road, she could see various cars and jeeps parked up alongside a rocky granite verge, while a squad car blocked the entrance to a nearby woodland car park and pedestrian access to the trail.

The GFU van was ushered through to the parking area by a local uniform, while another guard moved the squad car back to give them room to enter, before blocking the entrance again.

A plain van they knew belonged to the State Pathologist's office was already parked up.

Reilly stepped out of the passenger door and was soon greeted by a local cop. 'Mark Jennings. Thanks for coming out so promptly.'

'What have we got exactly?' She looked around as they walked, trying to get her bearings.

'Body was found up there just off the trail path, amidst some pretty dense scrub. We had no choice but to clear a way in to get to it, but tried not to disturb anything too much either. I was at your lecture on crime scene preservation last year, so made sure we did everything by the book. Pathologist is already up there.'

'Great thanks. Who called in the circus then?' Reilly asked, indicating a congregation of a dozen or so onlookers in another corner of the car park. They were all dressed for mountain weather, some had walking poles, while others seemed to carry sticks as they stood around talking sombrely amongst themselves.

'Victims's family unfortunately. They're part of

the ongoing search party that's been operating in the area since that journo David Walsh went missing. First responders are having a bit of a job keeping them back.'

'So you're sure the victim is the missing guy?'

'Well, the general description fits, but to be honest, nobody is going to be able to pick the poor divil out in a line-up.'

Reilly didn't need to know any more. It wasn't always humans that messed up a crime scene. Corpses in the wild were at the mercy of the elements plus easy pickings for native animals.

She and Gary carried their equipment up the pathway.

As they reached the scene, the assistant state pathologist Colm Lee, had just finished up.

'Have a look and we'll talk after,' was all he muttered to her, living up to his reputation of being a man of few words.

Reilly picked her way through the freshly chopped-back scrub bordering the trail.

After ten meters or so, the terrain changed to a decidedly more forestry setting up ahead, with rows upon rows of spruce trees stretching out as far as the eye could see.

The location of the body was easy to spot, since a canopy had been tied between a couple of tree trunks for shelter, and crime scene tape stretched around the area in a wide arc, while two officers stood guard.

Stepping under the tape, she and Gary moved towards the base of a tree, where tarp sheeting had been placed loosely over the body.

As Gary lifted off the sheet, a couple of flies buzzed around nearby, as Reilly got her first glimpse of the spectacle concealed beneath.

A male figure lay propped against the tree in a near-foetal position. His hiking attire was brightly coloured and stood out amongst the dark green and brown surroundings. At first glance, it looked as though the guy had simply slumped against the tree and fallen asleep.

Reilly thought back to the initial report of foul play, but the absence of obvious interference was confusing her a little. The pathologist's demeanour just now had seemed weird too, but unfamiliar with Lee's working style, she'd put that down to his mannerism.

But as she rounded the body to get a view of the victim's face, Reilly instinctively recoiled. Her brain worked as she tried to fathom exactly what she was looking at.

The guy's eyelids were partially open, blood and sinew trailing down from them in a deeply macabre fashion, but it was the eyes themselves that drew all focus. She crouched down closer to get a better view in the dim light caused by the tree cover and tarpaulin overhead, then taken aback, quickly stood up again bringing her hand to her mask in disgust.

The victim's eyeballs were missing, but it seemed

as though something else - not immediately apparent - looked to have been forcefully inserted to replace them.

An eye for an eye...

'Bad?' Gary grimaced, approaching gingerly.

She shuddered. 'See for yourself...'

He stooped down and let out several profanities before standing back up, looking squarely at Reilly. Even with his mouth and nose masked she could see his revulsion mirrored her own.

'What the actual fuck?' Gary spat.

'My thoughts exactly...'

10

The detectives pressed the intercom button mounted on the wall outside Sean Shaughnessy's legal practice.

Chris had expected a plush corporate setup; fitting for such a notoriously successful high-flier. Instead, they were faced with a single clear glass door devoid of any signage, and an intercom that didn't even have the name of the practice listed.

Either side of the entryway were two commercial premises: a chip shop on one side and an off licence on the other.

The current chipper clientele stood nearby dressed in school uniforms, hungrily feasting on deep-friend lunches from boxes and brown paper bags; the heady aroma of vinegar on hot chips making even Chris's stomach growl.

So he could only imagine Kennedy's salivating.

His partner pressed the intercom button again as

clients from the second establishment wandered past, eyeing them suspiciously. They too carried lunch in brown bags; but of the liquid variety.

The speaker crackled and Chris struggled to hear the voice above the background din.

'Yes?'

'Detectives - looking to speak with Maura O'Donnell.'

'I'll buzz you in. Straight up the stairs, first door on the right,' the disembodied female voice instructed, and Kennedy pushed the door open as an audible buzz signalled grant of entry.

The two made their way upstairs and were greeted on the landing by a smartly-dressed middle-aged woman standing in the doorway, which opened onto a basic waiting area.

A row of worn leather couches lined one wall, with a coffee table and some magazines neatly stacked in the centre.

'Ms O'Donnell?' Chris ventured pleasantly. 'We spoke on the phone yesterday. I'm Chris Delaney and this is my partner Detective Kennedy,' he explained, as his companion duly nodded in acknowledgment.

'Come through to the office and please, call me Maura.'

They followed the legal secretary into a larger space containing two separate desks positioned at right angles to each other.

Chris guessed that Sean Shaughnessy's only office employee was in her late forties, but she looked much older, her eyes bloodshot. He wondered if this was from grief caused by the untimely death of her boss, or maybe a coke habit. Either was just as likely.

Maura stood in front of a desk that looked tidy and well-organised, with a computer on one side and a sophisticated phone system on the other.

Behind it, a large window looked out across the road to a row of standard four-bed suburban houses. To the right was a glass-panelled door with the words *Meeting Room* emblazoned across it.

All in all, your typical legal practice, were it not for the fact that Sean Shaughnessy was not your typical lawyer.

'First of all, our condolences,' Chris began. 'I'm sure yesterday's events came as a huge shock.' Maura nodded sadly and sniffed. 'We just wanted a quick chat if that's OK.'

'Why don't ye take a seat in the boardroom - can I get you coffee or tea?' she asked, opening the adjoining door through to the other room.

Inside, the walls were lined with bookcases housing rows of chunky legal hardback books. In the centre was a rather antique-looking table with six matching chairs. On it and in front of each was a place setting with a thin leather writing mat, pen and two bottles of Ballygowan water; one still the other sparkling.

Chris wasn't sure if the place was so organised because it wasn't used very often, or if Maura or perhaps the recently-deceased Sean, was just a stickler for detail.

'We're fine, not long after a cuppa thanks,' he said, looking around the room at some of the books which he figured had never even been read. They each pulled out a seat each a sat down.

'I'll just close this door over altogether. Sorry about the noise - the phone has been constant all morning,' Maura said, referring to the various beeps and buzzes that had been going since they arrived.

Then she sat down, all business. 'So you have some questions. I have plenty myself, so perhaps we can enlighten each other,' she continued, sitting down opposite the detectives.

Her voice was firm and as she looked directly from one man to the other, Chris knew that she was not the type to be easily intimidated.

'I'm sure you have,' Kennedy said. 'But first, do you mind starting by telling us about Sean's movements yesterday?'

'There isn't really much to tell to be honest. I was here in the office first, around eight thirty and he arrived about nine. We were both preparing files for a court case starting today. I was just about to make us a coffee around eleven when he got a house alarm notification on his phone. He wasn't too concerned; it was a windy day so he just assumed the weather had set it off again. He left at about 11:10 at a guess, said he'd spin down to the house to sort it and then pick up two coffees on his way back.'

Chris took some notes as she spoke, underlining the mention of 'again'.

'We'll need the details of that court case you mentioned, just in case of any relevance,' he told her.

'I doubt it - it's just a straightforward insurance thing,' she said. 'But of course.'

'The house is what ... a mile or so away, maybe five minutes drive, tops from here?' Kennedy asked.

She nodded. 'Depends on traffic of course, but yes, around that time you'd usually be there and back in about ten minutes.'

'So at what point did you suspect there was something wrong?'

'Not for a while to be honest. I was expecting himself back before twelve, but it wouldn't be unusual for him to get sidetracked or waylaid by a call or what-have-you. I phoned, but it went straight to message minder so I figured he was on a call at the time. After a bit longer, I was starting to wonder if maybe it wasn't a false house alarm this time so I tried phoning him again. By the time lunchtime came around and I still couldn't get him, I was about to phone the local station when I got a call from a friend who'd ... heard the awful news.' She put a hand up to her throat and shook her head, as if still in disbelief.

Chris continued to write in his notebook as he turned the timeline over in his head, while Kennedy probed further.

'This 'friend' - was it someone in law enforcement, or media even?' he asked.

'Neither,' she replied, looking confused by the question.

'It's just that news of the incident would have been very low key at that stage. Barring emergency services and a few reporters with ears to the ground, not a lot of people would have been aware of Sean's ... situation.'

Maura's mouth tightened a little. 'This particular... person is local and when something happens in such circles, they tend to know about it,' she said.

'Can you give us a name? Perhaps this person could be of assistance,' Chris asked.

'Maybe, but I'd rather my name is kept out of it ...'

'Thats no problem, we'll be canvassing extensively throughout our investigation anyway,' Kennedy said in reassurance. 'No stone left unturned.'

She sighed. 'Jim Lynch called me. I'm sure you're aware of him?'

Chris looked up, unable to hide his surprise at the mention of a senior member of one of Dublin's most notorious criminal organisations. Though it wasn't just the name that caught his attention, but Maura's description of Lynch as a 'friend'.

'OK, well that makes more sense. Wouldn't be unusual for Jimmy to have his finger on the pulse. We'll have a chat, and don't worry we'll be discreet,' Kennedy soothed, hoping to appease the woman whose steely demeanour was gradually beginning to strain.

'Were there any direct threats made to Mr Shaughnessy recently that you're aware of, Maura?' Chris asked then.

She exhaled heavily. 'Lookit, it's no secret Sean had some high profile clients from the entertainment industry, as well as some other more ... questionable characters. Plus a very active social life and business connections generally,' she added, evidently knowing better than to try to play down her boss's reputation. 'And yes, while of course he's been involved in some high-profile cases recently, as far as I know there was never any plausible threat made against him.'

'What about implausible threats then?' Kennedy asked. 'We're open to all avenues.'

She made a face. 'He always gets a few nasty emails and some stuff said about him online all right, but like I said nothing that would cause undue concern.'

'Might you have any records of those?'

She nodded. 'Sean was no fool - he kept everything. He has a file in one of his drawers marked 'fan mail' actually.'

'It'd be very helpful to take a look at those if we may. Ideally, we'd also like copies of ongoing client files from the past couple of years.' Given she was being so co-operative, Chris decided to chance his arm.

Maura looked at him. 'I don't see any issue with the fan mail since that's not directly client related, but I would need to take advisement on the other - just to follow protocol, you understand.'

'Of course, we can make a more formal request for information if that makes it easier.'

'Yes, that would be useful for compliance on my end, even though I'm not sure how long I'll be here now. This is a solo practice, and with Sean gone it's ...' she trailed off, looking pained afresh.

'Maura, again many thanks for your time,' Chris said, beginning to wrap things up. 'There was one thing you mentioned earlier about the house alarm - you implied it going off was a regular thing?'

'Yes, according to Sean it just seemed to be a bit temperamental lately. Never happened before until a few weeks back, and then he was getting one or two alerts a week - figured it was a malfunction or something,' she mused, as they all stood and made their way back into the main office.

Malfunction ... Chris wondered dubiously. Or strategic desensitisation?

11

Back in the GFU lab, Lucy was still sifting through the evidence from the Shaughnessy scene to in order to start categorising and processing.

The image of the crime lawyer's smoking, smouldering torso had popped into her head too many times since yesterday.

She didn't know how Reilly always seemed to take these things in her stride, but her boss never seemed to flinch.

At anything.

Even now, she was back on the job as if nothing at all had happened. Granted, the woman rarely ever showed any sign of being fragile, but what had happened with the baby was bound to have affected her surely?

She shook her head. While Lucy worshipped the

ground her boss and mentor walked on, Reilly Steel had always been a conundrum - to all of them.

She looked at the bundle of evidence bags spread out on her work station, trying to decide what to work on next.

Footprint casings, a discarded half-eaten apple, duct tape from the meter box and a fried iPhone - ready to dispatch to the cyber unit once they'd cleared it for trace.

Deciding that duct tape was always a good idea, she picked up a single bag and brought it over to the microscope at the opposite end of the work station.

Making sure her hair was fully tucked inside standard issue hairnet, Lucy perched on the stool in front of the apparatus and brought the sample closer for cursory examination.

Part of the tape had become partially stuck to itself at one end during its application, but she could clearly spy what she hoped would be their first piece of differentiated evidence.

A single strand of brown hair sat embedded in the adhesive coating. Holding the swab in one hand Lucy swung the light arm of the scope so she could illuminate the tape, while looking through the magnifying glass.

Slightly disappointed, she pushed the light away and rolled her chair sideways towards the scope, deciding to just place the tape itself under the lens rather than trying to separate the hair from it. As she turned the dials to focus in, it didn't take long to confirm the reason for her initial disappointment; the immediate absence of a hair root.

'Shite,' she muttered, louder than she had intended, causing Julius to look up from nearby.

'What's up?' her colleague asked.

'Hair from the tape, it's synthetic.'

He shrugged. 'Still might come in useful.'

'Not as useful as if it was real, and we could eke some DNA from it.'

'As if was ever going to be that easy,' he chuckled.

'How long? I mean, is the sample short enough that it might not be hair at all?'

'Nah, too long I reckon. And sure what else could it be?'

'Extensions, wigs again....' Julius let his guesses hang.

'Hope not,' Lucy grimaced, recalling a recent macabre case involving wigs - and as it turned out, her very own sister. 'OK so we know whoever rigged that place did it in broad daylight - perhaps using a disguise?'

They both pondered this for a moment. But of course it was way too early for assumptions at this point, she knew. Like starting a jigsaw and expecting to see where a single piece fit into the overall picture.

'Anyway, take a look at this and tell me what you think,' Julius then gestured to the assembled casts and shoe imprints he was working on. 'Check out the sizes,' he prompted, pushing his notes into her field of vision, whereupon there were several calculations and the figure "39" written at the bottom and underlined. 'Could tie in with the disguise thing couldn't it?'

'Very small shoe size ...' she commented, and he nodded.

'Exactly. Hell hath no fury like a woman scorned?'

THE WORDS KEPT GOING through Lucy's mind as later that day, she drove to the city mortuary. Her workload throughout Reilly's recent absence had been heavy and she was starting to feel it.

She was unsure if it was just the fact her mentor was back and she could ease off a little that was making her feel so tired. As if the adrenaline of the extra responsibility had been keeping her going. But now she felt as fatigued as she could ever remember.

She indicated to pull into the car park while waiting for a group of joggers to move past the entrance. Seeing their lycra-clad legs tottering past, caused her to think of her imbalanced work situation.

Though at least Gary understood that better than any other guy would, and while they didn't have a whole lot of free time as a couple, they seemed to be managing to make their relationship work so far.

Despite her fatigue, Lucy was as happy as she'd ever been really. She and her dad had come to an impasse about her working in the forensic unit, and life in general was looking up.

She just needed to ensure that she didn't follow Reilly's lead in making the job the absolute centre of her world. Because she knew that couldn't be good for anyone in the long run, least of all her boss.

Glancing at the joggers, a cop joke she'd once heard jumped into her head: *My only source of exercise is jumping to conclusions.*

Lucy's mind automatically drifted back to that morning's work and her conversation with Julius.

Did small feet and fake hair indicate a female suspect, or was she jumping to conclusions.

'Men kill by violence, women by stealth,' Reilly had once pointed out.

A broad generalisation of motive and method differentiating male and female killers, Lucy knew. But typically, if a woman was driven to murder, she needed to rely on something other than brute physicality.

Whereas the opposite sex could easily kill on impulse and rage - and more often than not, did exactly that.

Thinking back on her time at the GFU so far, so few of the brutal cases she'd worked had been committed by women. Apart from one particularly memorable one not long after Reilly had taken over.

But that had been the exception really.

There had been quite a few crimes of passion, where loved-ones argued and the male partner had ended up at the wrong end of a sharp instrument - even a stiletto in one memorable instance. And countless female domestic abuse victims who'd plotted the downfall of their abuser via absent means.

Whereas the Sean Shaughnessy case was different. It was more direct; bold and gratuitous and clearly designed to cause maximum suffering.

Lucy tried to keep an open mind, but the conclusion she'd already jumped to was that if the doer did happen to be female, then they were surely looking for an ex lover, or someone Shaughnessy had done wrong by.

The lawyer's reputation as a notorious womaniser suggested that list may well be as long as her arm.

She slammed the car door shut and pressed the lock button on her key fob as she swallowed hard, bracing herself for her reacquaintance with Shocks Shaughnessy, deep in the bowels of the mortuary.

While his nickname had derived from the lawyer's courtroom antics, Lucy'd also heard a similar moniker applied to the man's charismatic presence - electric.

Was the use of voltage as a means of dispatch in this case coincidentally ironic, or blatantly intentional?

12

'Put that back, you know that's for emergencies only.' Cici reached across to take the can of pineapples from her sister.

'It is an emergency - I'm hungry.' Emmy ran laughing through the door of the twelve by twelve-foot room lined with floor to ceiling storage shelves heaving with jars and tins. And bottles of that funny water that used to make Papa so crazy.

'It's not funny, you know. Mama will smack you if she finds out,' she chided.

'Ah, don't be such a goody-two-shoes - one won't be missed; there are loads in there.' Her younger sister stood in the doorway looking longingly at the fruit picture on the can. 'Let's share it.'

Cici caught up with her and yanked the tin from her grasp.

'No. You *know* we can't eat the food in here. Remember what Mama always says ...'

'Yeah, yeah, one day a handful of rice will be worth more than a bar of gold.' She rolled her eyes. 'Well, I'm hungry *now* and we have a room full of this stuff.' She pointed to rows upon rows of neatly stacked non-perishable foods, all labelled with meticulous care.

Papa always said he'd keep them safe, protect them from all evil until the day the earth would cure itself.

He had lived most of his life getting ready for it; shunning modern ways. He'd studied how-to books on water purifying and generating electricity.

And they had spent all of their lives preparing for it too.

Their parents were teaching the girls everything they would need to survive - not in the world as it was, Cici knew, but the one that was yet to come. Teaching them how to endure until the very end.

Whatever that meant.

13

Chris opened his eyes and stared at the red glow cast by his alarm clock.

He felt like he had only closed his eyes seconds ago. Yesterday had been a long one, and today would be even longer.

He rolled onto his side and sat up in the bed groaning as his joints ached.

Prioritising Reilly's needs so much lately meant that he'd let things slide - irregular meals, lack of sleep and exercise were making him feel tired and weary.

Though maybe not as much as rejection did.

But he also knew the aching joints were more likely related to his haemochromatosis, and the fact that he needed to let blood more regularly to help ease the inevitable iron build-up in his system.

But lately, he hadn't been as diligent about that as he should be.

Gingerly, he pushed himself up and headed into the ensuite to take a leak, before jumping into the shower in the hope the hot water would loosen him up a bit.

After dressing and grabbing some toast and a coffee, he headed for the door, trying to process how best to approach what was happening this morning.

He'd hoped to discuss all this with Reilly the other night over dinner, but the evening had not exactly gone as planned.

To put it mildly.

Well, maybe that was no harm. This was something that he and he alone needed to figure out.

There was simply no point in even thinking about trying to figure Reilly Steel into his plans anymore. She'd made that patently clear.

They'd been doing this dance for way too long as it was.

And while he still felt for everything she was going through right now, and would continue to support her however she wanted (or allowed), as far as he was concerned he'd done his bit.

Gone above and beyond even, because as far as Chris was concerned, he and Reilly had always had each other's backs as partners, friends, whatever.

And he'd hoped that maybe sometime in the future, once the dust settled, they could even be something more.

But she'd since made it painfully clear that she

didn't see things that way. And once again Chris felt like an idiot.

He was kidding himself to think that they were making progress, that there was any hope of progressing their relationship beyond whatever it was now.

So maybe it was about time he started to focus on himself.

A LITTLE WHILE LATER, Chris parked his car outside Garda HQ in the Phoenix Park, and turned off the ignition. Reaching over to the passenger seat, he pulled out a white envelope from the inside pocket of his jacket.

He looked at his watch; ten minutes early. Then pulled the document from the envelope and re-read the words for probably the tenth time.

The first time he'd read the letter a couple of weeks back, he'd scanned and dismissed all out of hand - though he had to admit he was intrigued.

By the fifth time he read it, he was flattered and beginning to visualise what it could be like, and what he might do differently from those that had gone before.

To say nothing of the fact that he'd been considering settling down and prioritising a quieter life in any case. Life on the streets was beginning to get him down, and physically he wasn't sure he was really able for it anymore.

It didn't mean that he'd be any less of a cop - more that this was an opportunity to tackle law enforcement differently. Which given the way his life (and health) seemed to be going, was starting to make more and more sense.

A change of scenery might be a good thing, especially now.

Could he really dismiss an opportunity that didn't come along very often, and may never come along again if he didn't properly consider it?

Though having read the contents again while waiting to go inside, Chris was soon back at stage one - flat-out rejection.

The thought of giving up fieldwork, of saying goodbye to the Serious Crime team he'd worked so closely with for the last seven years, frightened him.

Though the thought of working his way up along the ladder within the higher echelons and all the political bullshit that came with that, scared him too.

But it wasn't just fear; there was something else, a burning question that had been echoing in his head more and more lately; where was he going?

That idea had presented itself even stronger after the other night. And the answer was obvious; he was going around in circles.

His jaw working, Chris got out of the car, slammed the door and made his way into reception.

After waiting outside a conference room for a couple of minutes, his name was called and he rose to his feet. Walking through the open door to where four senior Garda officials were waiting, he greeted them and closed the door behind him.

Realising that each step he took was ultimately a step away from the job he had dedicated his life to for far too long.

And perhaps just as importantly, Chris thought determinedly, helping to put some distance once and for all between him and Reilly Steel.

14

'I think we'll have to get you guys an office over here,' Reilly said, in an attempt to break the strained silence when the detectives arrived at the GFU to go over preliminary findings from the Sean Shaughnessy scene.

'I hear we're going to be seeing a lot more of each other, all right,' Kennedy grumbled from the doorway of her office.

'Oh I meant to say before, tell Josie thanks for the card,' she told him, the thought coming to her out of the blue. 'Unnecessary but kind all the same.'

Though when the big man reddened up uncomfortably, she regretted saying anything.

But it was the truth. Given the circumstances, such gestures *were* unnecessary. Like Doctor Moore, Reilly's obstetrician had said, 'these things happened sometimes.'

And they did. Yes, the pregnancy being cut short

like that had been a shock and a disappointment, to say nothing of completely surreal. Especially when she'd had to break the news to Todd, who having been at the most recent ultrasound whereupon all was fine, couldn't understand what had gone wrong in the interim.

Neither could she.

Her obstetrician had reeled off a list of potential causations and was currently investigating any heretofore unknown or underlying medical issues.

But none of that could change the outcome, so what did it matter?

Again, these things happened.

'Why don't you go grab some coffee and head into the conference room - give us a few minutes to get everything together?'

She was also doing her utmost to avoid Chris's gaze but soon realised she didn't need to. He was behaving as if they didn't even know one another.

OK.

Clearly he was still pissed about the other night. Which wasn't fair given the day they'd both had, and the fact that Reilly just wasn't up to discussing her emotional state anymore.

Time to move on.

'OK, let's get started,' she began, once the entire team had assembled in the conference room. She indicated to an empty cork board and then nodded at Gary.

'First up, shoe treads from Shock ... I mean, the

Sean Shaughnessy scene, sorry,' he said backtracking at her disapproving frown, as he began to affix various reports, photographic images and tread imprints on the board. 'Some decent tread from inside the house, the external stuff was only useful for sizing, really. Relatively small; European 39, which is a size 6 - possibly even smaller. The inside prints are more revealing.' He indicated a photo that had been zoomed-in and enhanced. 'Tread marks are distinctive on this one in particular. You can also make out the brand name in the mid sole area.'

'Vibram. Running shoes?' Chris pondered out loud, evidently familiar with the brand.

'More likely hiking boots,' Gary confirmed. 'Vibram is indeed a type of running shoe but they primarily produce soles for hiking. Tread is deep, too deep for road running. I narrowed down the brand of boot that uses these particular soles, so we should be able to fine-tune further with regard to manufacturer and suppliers. Luckily, these are a pretty specialist thing, so with a bit of luck we might be able to pinpoint an actual retailer before long.'

'Right. So a hiker with tiny feet who likes to play with electricity wires,' Kennedy drawled.

'Could make sense if one of Shaughnessy's 'connections' got a couple of his minions to do his dirty work, so to speak?' Chris ventured.

'Pretty elaborate set-up though. Organised crime gangs doesn't usually deal in this kind of theatrics,'

Reilly mused. 'Wouldn't it be easier to just walk up to the guy and shoot him at the door?'

'True enough. Anything else to go on then?'

To her relief, Chris didn't seem to take any umbrage at the counterargument. Good, the last thing she needed was having to walk on eggshells around him because his ego was bruised.

Though to be fair, he'd never been like that. When it came to an investigation anyway.

Gary picked up another folder. 'Still working on a lot of it, but I did manage to isolate some gritty, as yet unidentified organic material that could have become dislodged from the treads. It will take a while to individuate, but fingers crossed.'

'Great. Lucy you also got something from the duct tape?' Reilly looked at the younger tech.

'Yes, bit of a dead end though - literally so. At first I thought we'd got a good hair sample with follicle intact but turned out to be synthetic. Not going to tell us a whole lot in its own right.'

'What about the autopsy?' she asked, once again relieved she'd been able to duck out on that one because of the more recent missing journalist find.

'Nasty,' Chris said grimacing. 'Official cause of death was heart failure due to electrocution, which is no surprise. M.E. estimates he was exposed to the current before the melted skin broke away and he fell to the ground. Multiple dislocations caused by severe muscle spasms. She's sending across a full report, along with the tox screen, his clothes and the usual. You already have his phone, which must surely yield something provided it wasn't barbecued too.'

'No, seems like he was holding it in the other hand and dropped it with the jolt from the handle. Rory's working on extracting the data.'

'One thing for sure - whoever set up all that was pretty calm and calculated,' Lucy mused. 'Hard not to think it's all about the company the man keeps.'

'Maybe even more calculated than we first thought,' Chris said.

'How so?'

'Seems that the alarm had been tripped on several occasions over the last few weeks according to the secretary. Had become a nuisance rather than a warning. So if whoever broke in knew how long it would take Sean Shaughnessy to respond to the alarm, they had a timeline for getting everything set up.'

'And have the neighbours complaining about the noise rather than suspect a burglary in progress,' Kennedy pointed out.

'Clever. Anything else from the secretary?'

'Just a couple of leads to chase up. One of the Lynches broke the bad news apparently,' Chris said, rolling his eyes.

'*The* Lynches,' Reilly's eyes widened, though again this was hardly a surprise, given this victim's well-established organised crime connections. But something about all this didn't scream garden variety gangland crime hit. It seemed way too elaborate for them to bother.

This one seemed personal.

'We're looking into accessing some of his legal files, but I don't know if the request will stand up as yet. The secretary also mentioned he's had some negative press in the past, so we're going to check that out too.'

'Speaking of press, is it true what they've being saying about that journo?' Kennedy asked. 'You were up there the other day, I hear.'

'Yes. It ... wasn't pretty.'

'Something about apples in his eyes ... what the hell is all that about?'

'Your guess is as good as mine.' But then Reilly paused, suddenly remembering something. She looked at the detectives. 'Did the M.E. mention anything in particular about Shaughnessy's stomach contents?'

'Nothing especially memorable, why?'

'Probably nothing, but I just remember he looked to have been munching on an apple before he entered the house. There was one lying by the body with a bite taken out of it.'

Chris looked thoughtful. 'The secretary did say he was going to bring them back something for a coffee break - but an apple seems an odd choice.'

'Unless yer man is one of those fitness weirdos? Going for the real thing instead of an apple turnover,' Kennedy quipped. 'Or is that the other way round?'

Lucy was flicking through pages. 'That's right, I have it listed here. Apple with a single bite taken out of it. Do you want to run bite mark or saliva comparison ... ?'

'Dunno - just thinking out loud, really. And yes,' she said, replying to Kennedy. 'David Walsh's eyes were removed and replaced with a couple of apples. Eyeballs still haven't been found as yet.'

The big man gulped. 'That's it. I'm never biting into one again.'

15

A little later, Chris slowed the car as the traffic lights changed from amber to red. Two youths walked along the footpath; hoods over their heads as they led a dishevelled horse along the grass verge between the road and the path.

The green on the far side was a patchwork of scorch marks where small fires had been lit - dark black earth with the solidified plastic molten remains of what was once household wheelie bins set alight to keep the night dwellers of 'The Valley' warm after dark.

The nickname given to several high density housing estates in North Dublin, it was an area of stark contrasts.

Out of its crime filled, drug-riddled streets had come some of the country's greatest sports stars, kids who had used their disadvantaged backgrounds as motivation to get out.

On the flip side, for every impoverished kid who had made something of themselves, dozens more went on to live normal, unremarkable lives without drama. But there was also a high number of residents that chose a life of petty crime and drug addiction - and an even greater majority evolving to lesser again.

Most of these ended up being schooled and employed by the dominant criminal gang in the vicinity, the Lynch family.

At the top of food chain was Jim Lynch, a notorious thug who had earned his badges on the city streets, and one of eight brothers who had all been involved in crime thanks to a longstanding family tradition.

Having seen his father and uncles fall victim to turf feuds and drug taking, and witnessed the demise of some of his elder brothers, Jim had resolved to revolutionise the family 'business.'

He had eradicated two rival organisations; assimilating the remaining members, and set up legal business interests, employing an army of loyal minions among local disenfranchised youths.

Using these kids to do his dirty work, Lynch had built an empire and kept his hands clean, thanks in no small part to his friend, confidant and legal representative, Sean Shaughnessy.

As the traffic lights turned, Chris pulled off and

the group eyed the unmarked car, fully aware of who they were.

He stared right back as they eyeballed him on the way past, unafraid to make eye contact. Undoubtedly they had already sent alerts and made calls about 'pigs' in the area.

Further down the road, he pulled into a parking area beside an ugly eighties-built building with the ground floor windows shuttered off, and graffiti covering the steel shutters and walls.

An old sign at the top of the building read 'The Valley Boxing Club' and underneath, a newer printed sign; *'Congratulations Billy O'Neill, European Middleweight Champion.'*

Indicating one of Jim Lynch's passion projects that did inspire hope and give an outlet for local youth in the area, but Chris knew it could never atone for everything else the guy stood for.

'What time did he say he'd meet us?' he asked, as they parked up close to a front door which operated in two parts, the first was a heavy steel contraption that closed over an inner timber door.

Nobody gained access here uninvited.

'Said he'd be here all evening, that's his car there I'd say,' Kennedy nodded toward a high end Mercedes SUV that sat highly polished and pristine in the corner, not the kind of car people parked in this area. Only those with a death wish would dare harm or steal a Lynch motor.

Chris got out, closed his door and walked around,

smelling fresh cigarette smoke coming out the slightly-opened window.

No doubt the boss already knew he had visitors.

'You know what I find mad?' Kennedy said in hushed tones as he walked alongside Chris. 'All the money spent on sport in this country, millions, billions even, over the space of a couple of decades,' He looked up at the signage above the front door. 'This place has seen four Olympic medals pass through its doors in that time, including Ireland's only gold, yet this place looks fit for a wrecking ball.'

'It's a strange one all right,' Chris said as they moved towards the door.

'Just goes to show that money doesn't win golds, hunger does.' Kennedy continued, somewhat prophetically as he pushed down the interior door handle.

Inside, their senses were assaulted by the ripe stench of sweat and muscle ointment. The large hall opened out in front of them with four full size boxing rings evenly spaced in the centre.

Toward the back was a series of punchbags and balls of various shapes and sizes; young wiry, tattooed young guys working the bags while receiving instruction from various not so wiry but equally tattooed coaches.

There was a notable energy encircling the room. The noise of leather against leather and rubber against rubber as young kids were put through their paces, practicing their footwork while coordinating their jabs.

The left hand side of the room was the weight section. Kids worked in pairs 'spotting' each other as they worked the irons.

Chris was almost surprised at the level of focus - nobody even raised an eye to them. In any other situation around here, a detective's entrance would be very different.

He glanced at Kennedy who nodded towards the other side of the room as he started to walk around the perimeter of the hall.

As Chris followed he noticed the men seated against a wall, watching closely as two men sparred inside a boxing ring.

He recognised a couple of faces immediately, including that of Jim Lynch. As they approached he noted the older gentlemen sitting with the notorious crime lord, looked like extras from a mobster movie as they silently watched the sparring match.

The noise of gloves making contact with skin and skullcaps, and boxers expelling air as they swung and jabbed, was surprisingly loud to Chris who, unlike Kennedy, had only ever seen boxing on television.

His partner took the lead, being more familiar with Jim Lynch and his ilk than he was.

'Mind if we have that chat you promised me?' Kennedy asked raising his voice in order to be audible over the din. Jim raised a single finger, not taking his eyes off the two fighters who continued to dance around the ring trading blows.

'Stand off him - you're coming inside too much,' he growled at the kid.

The detectives stood patiently and watched as the referee or coach in the ring with the two boys, stepped in to push them apart as they grappled with each other trying to find the room to swing another punch.

Chris wasn't sure if Jim was enjoying making them wait, or he just cared more about the sparring. After another minute or so he stood up and cupped his hands together to call time.

'Right lads, take a breather for five and then hit the bags.'

The two fighters duly stopped and bumped their gloves together to acknowledge each others' efforts as they removed their gum shields and walked off.

'Gents, what can I do for you?' Jim asked politely, as he led the detectives to the side.

'Sean Shaughnessy. As mentioned, I'd like to pick your brains,' Kennedy reminded him.

'Yeah, just not sure how I can help.'

'You and the deceased were friends, yes?' Chris asked.

'That we were, I was gutted when I heard what happened to poor old Shocks. Shitty way to go considering.'

'Did he mention anything unusual? Anybody giving him hassle recently?'

'Not that I know of, or at least not any more guff than usual. Anything serious he'd have told me.'

'You just said when you heard about it you were gutted, how did you find out?'

'Can't remember. News like that travels fast.'

'I suppose you're right, Maura in the office seems to have found out pretty quickly too - she can't remember who told her either.'

'Like I said, things like that don't stay quiet for long. Shocks was a good friend, and before you ask I don't know who is responsible for what happened - if I did believe me I'd have no problem setting you right. Even though your crowd seem hell-bent on looking to me and my business every time you can't do your job properly.'

'Steady on Jim, we are trying to do our job. Seems we're on the same side for once,' Kennedy said.

'See, there you go again. Fuck your same side. When will you shower realise I'm not the fucking enemy here. So why don't you fuck off and find out who is instead of hassling me. You're barking up the wrong tree.'

Chris attempted to lower the temperature by steering the conversation onto matters other than Jim's business interests.

'What about any lady friends? Was Sean seeing anyone that might have had reason to be ... upset with him?'

Jim laughed. 'I'd say there's no shortage of those to be fair. But none that'd have the gumption to ...

well, you know yourself. Most of Shock's women didn't have much upstairs either - apart from the missus of course. And balls to measure.'

Chris noticed the guy's voice and demeanour changed considerably now.

'Ex-wife I believe?' he clarified. 'Unless there's a future Mrs Shaughnessy we need to know about ...'

'One is enough for anyone, that one especially,' the crime boss grunted, and walked back towards the ring where two fresh fighters were now starting to spar, signalling that the meeting was over.

Once outside, the fresh air and calm was noticeable after the cacophony noise and smells inside.

'You think he really suspects the ex's involvement or is he just acting the maggot?' he asked Kennedy.

'Who knows ... Be interesting to pay her a visit all the same. Not many people I know - least of all a woman - who'd rattle the likes of Jim Lynch.'

He'd definitely seemed rattled all right, Chris thought.

Must be something in the air...

They ambled back to the Ford to see a couple of young lads no more than eight or nine, standing alongside it.

'Hey mister, I like your motor. We're just after stopping a lad from jacking it,' said one.

'Yeah you're lucky we were here or you'd be walking home,' the other added.

'Cheers lads, we owe ye one.'

'Give us a tenner and we're quits.'

'You must be joking...'

'Show us your gun then.'

'Yeah, show us your badge.'

'C'mon lads, it's a school night - shouldn't ye be at home?'

'School... fuck school,' the younger one said, looking directly at Chris, the level of brazenness not surprising him. Kids around here were taught not to fear anybody, least of all cops.

'Yeah Damo lets go, tight pigs definitely won't pay up.' The other broke into a sprint and the two of them ran off, laughing and calling insults over their shoulders.

Kennedy shook his head as he got into the passenger seat. 'No bloody respect ... if we'd done that when I was a kid you'd have got a hiding and my 'oul fella would've shaken the cops' hand for putting manners on us.'

'Yeah well, it wouldn't do those little shits any harm either,' he agreed, turning the key in the ignition. 'What the ...?' Then he trailed off and killed the engine, putting it back in neutral.

'What's up?' Kennedy asked.

'Little bastards ...' Chris groaned, getting back out to tackle the Ford's suddenly pancake-flat rear tyre.

16

Reilly moved her legs slowly, then picked up the pace, feeling her muscles yell in pain as she tried to concentrate on her breathing while trying to deal with the cold, her brain unable to focus on anything else other than to keep moving.

Her motivation to exercise had all but vanished of late; her abandoned trainers on the floor in the flat taunting her every time she passed them.

Running had always acted as a tool to bring equilibrium to her life. A means to think calmly and reflect on whatever was going on at the time.

Lately though, she didn't want to think; fearful of where her mind might wander.

Which is why it had been so important to go back to work as soon as was physically possible.

As she controlled her breathing and relaxed a little, familiar, unsettling thoughts - the very ones she needed to escape from - began to once again drift into her consciousness.

She took another gulp of air and pushed harder, kicking her legs and rotating her arms as she pushed away the icy cold water.

Here, there were only two choices available; sink or swim.

Reilly cut through the waters of Dublin Bay, parallel to the shore heading south away from Seapoint Beach, where she had entered.

The stone Martello tower and bathing shelters by the water's edge were busy with other sea swimmers, some enjoying a post-swim warm-up by way of flasks of hot coffee as they sat shivering on the rocks in towels or dry-robes.

She'd started to recognise a couple of familiar faces since she had first ventured down here a couple of weeks ago.

There was something about sea-swimming in particular; the expressions others wore emerging from the utterly chilling water was mostly one of calm and contentedness.

These people were present; at one with nature, as opposed to scrolling on mobile devices or rushing off somewhere.

The nods of acknowledgment seemed to come from a place of understanding - a not so secret club of people who'd rediscovered a way of connecting with what it truly meant to feel alive.

Reilly approached the rocks that normally

marked her turnaround point and was struck by a sense of liberation. When she ran, there was too much opportunity to think; her body on autopilot. And lately, she'd been feeling confined by roads and walls and buildings, travelling in pre-determined loops that meant she was merely going round in circles. Always ending up right back where she started.

Not too unlike her life in general.

Here though in the ocean, she was free to go wherever she wanted, to keep on moving for as long as she could. She didn't even need to turn at the rocks; she could just swim around them, keep on going off into the horizon for as long as her body could take it.

Hell, the only thing between her and home was thousands of miles of ocean. Though deciding against a dramatic US transatlantic crossing, she turned and headed back towards the now sunlit stone tower.

She kicked harder, realising she'd gone under a little once land-based thoughts had filled her mind, and quite literally dragged her down.

Sink or swim.

Pushing on a little faster, until eventually reaching waist-deep water closer to shore, she eventually grabbed the old, rusty handrail and emerged from the depths - her legs wobbling unsteadily beneath her as they readjusted to bearing vertical weight.

She walked awkwardly up the concrete steps, teeth chattering and leg muscles stiff from the effort and cold, and made her way to a bench nearby where she'd left her things.

'Beautiful morning for it,' an older lady sitting a little way down called out as Reilly approached.

She gave a faint smile and nodded, unwilling to engage in conversation or become part of the tribe just yet.

Much like running, the solo element of this particular activity was part of the attraction.

One thing she wasn't a fan of though, was trying to strip off a freezing, soaked wetsuit when her hands were cold and numb, so she just sat and waited for the blood to flow back into her fingers, watching the waves gently lap against the shore.

Other swimmers exited and entered the water nearby, the majority considerably older, and a few considerably tougher given they didn't feel the need to wear a wetsuit in the freezing waters of the bay.

The sun rose even higher in the sky, and she placed her back against the concrete wall behind, and lifted her face up to bask in the light.

Then watched with interest as a younger girl entered the water and exited again just as quickly, barely getting wet as she held out her phone, taking several selfie shots in the early morning sunlight. Reilly knew the pictures would soon be filtered to perfection and posted online in a lot less time than the girl had spent in the water.

#goldenhour

She closed her eyes again and let the sun illuminate her own face as her recharged mind drifted. So much of society's concerns right now stemmed from the inability to be present in the moment, much like that girl. The younger generation's increasingly overwhelming desire to live life in a virtual realm continuously seeking validation from strangers, made her feel tired and old, and she felt bad for any parent who had to contend with it.

Maybe it was indeed all for the best that Reilly didn't need to worry about anything like that just yet.

If ever.

17

Later that evening, she stood decked-out in a white gown and face mask, topped off with a standard issue pale green hairnet.

The relief she'd experienced upon avoiding Sean Shaughnessy's autopsy earlier this week, was matched by the dread she was feeling now.

The routine practice of a senior GFU member being present for observation at autopsy - and one she herself had been instrumental in introducing - was not lost on her.

And so now Reilly watched, notepad and pen in hand, as Dr Colm Lee - the pathologist she'd met at the crime scene, and his mortuary assistant - prepared the body of the since-identified journalist, David Walsh; his corpse laid-out on the slab.

She was glad at least that it wasn't Karen Thompson - another sympathetic face would be too much. While the doc had also sent a card and a floral bouquet, Reilly was relieved to avoid any awkward face to face condolences.

Now, she tried to divert her gaze from Walsh's face as the assistant pulled a sheet over his torso to allow Colm Lee to systematically work through his initial visual observation.

'Ready to proceed?' The doctor looked to his audience, comprised of Reilly and a couple of local officers, joined also by three pathology students, all standing silently poised to observe the grim spectacle.

Everybody nodded and the M.E. duly pressed a button on his voice recorder and placed it in a small breast pocket that looked as though it could have been specifically designed for that use.

Then read off a couple of reference numbers from a clipboard, before placing it aside and rolling down the top of the sheet to reveal the victim's head, neck and shoulders.

'Commencing initial physical examination of Mr David Walsh.'

Having rattled off the victim's confirmed personal stats, the doctor proceeded to observe and comment on the appearance of his corpse. He moved his head around, using a small flash-light to illuminate ear, nose and mouth areas, describing his observations as he went.

Reilly noted how he'd referred to the fast-decaying fruit still positioned in Walsh's eye sockets, as 'yet unidentified foreign objects,' as per protocol.

'Lividity has occurred in the lower torso and posterior areas, suggesting the subject passed in a sitting or crouched position.'

'Subject's wrists are badly cut and chaffed from plastic cable tie binding, indicating repeated attempts by the subject to break free from it,' the doctor continued, his voice low as he reached for a tweezer and pulled at some loose skin around the wrist area.

'Also some major contusions running perpendicular to these markings, which appears to have been caused by debris, embedded with some organic material. Without speculating, and in advance of further analysis, this material has the appearance of wooden splinters - perhaps caused by the subject attempting to free his hands against a tree branch or with a wooden stick.' He removed several pieces of the aforementioned organic material and placed all into a clear plastic bag before sealing it.

Then Lee moved onto the next area.

'There are numerous small puncture marks and scratches on the chest skin. Some appear to resemble small pin pricks, consistent with more pronounced scratch marks on the face and neck. At this point, my hypothesis would be that such marks were caused by the victim stumbling through vegetation without the means to shield himself or indeed, ascertain his route.'

Reilly felt a shiver run down her spine. The mental picture the M.E. painted was of an isolated desperate figure, blind and alone, stumbling through a remote area, with no eyes to see and no hands to feel.

She couldn't begin to imagine the terror and could only hope for David Walsh's sake that he wasn't conscious when his eyes were being gouged out, or whatever means were used to remove them.

The doc continued his visual inspection, his words echoing around the morgue's cold interior. After reaching the toes he returned to the victim's head and proceeded with a more invasive examination.

Starting with the objects lodged in the journalist's eye sockets. Without hesitation, he picked up tongs from the stainless steel trolley positioned at the top of the slab and proceeded to deftly remove each apple from the eye socket.

Reilly heard an involuntary gasp from one of the medical students, and wouldn't have been altogether surprised if it had also been accompanied by involuntary projectile vomiting, such was the gruesome nature of what was unfolding.

'The foreign objects inserted in the eye sockets appear to be organic in nature,' the doctor continued, unperturbed by the reaction.

Reilly studied the overripe clump of fruit sitting in full view on the stainless steel tray.

A swirl of questions spun through her head.

That phrase, apples... apple of my eye? Apple of

his eyes? There had to be something symbolic about it.

David Walsh was a journalist. Was the doer perhaps trying to make some kind of point about what he chose to write about, about his objectivity?

Or lack thereof even.

In order to establish this line of enquiry, they needed to know more about the journalist and his line of work. Rory was already compiling a collection of Walsh's recent articles and anything else that might convey why he had been targeted in such a brutal manner.

The remainder of the autopsy continued without incident or surprise, and she watched impassively as the victim's organs were routinely weighed, examined and sampled before being returned to their owner.

It was a macabre ritual, and one she'd witnessed time and time again.

But as the M.E. finished up, Reilly now felt a little stupid for being initially dubious about observing here today - given her own more recent encounter with the stark realities of unexplained death.

Because much to her relief, she'd felt ... nothing.

18

Cici felt like somebody had thrown a bucket of cold water over her.

The feeling of being so deep in peaceful sleep and then being yanked violently from it made her sit up in bed, head spinning, trying to figure out what was happening.

The screaming got louder as she finally started to gather her senses, and she shuffled across to Emmy's bed.

'Shhhh. It's only a nightmare. It's OK, you're just dreaming again, you're OK,' she soothed, as her terrified little sister looked back at her with fear and anguish in her eyes.

Emmy's breathing slowed and the tide of panic ebbed as she sat up in the bed, her face wet from sweat and tears.

'It's OK, it's just another bad dream,' Cici reassured. Her younger sister wrapped her arms around her in relief as the tears continued to come. 'A bad one this time?' she asked.

Emmy didn't reply, knowing her words would be swallowed up by sobs. Instead she just nodded as she buried her face into her Cici's chest.

'It's OK, everything's OK.'

After a few more minutes, she seemed to recover.

'Do you want to talk about it?' Cici asked.

'It was a man, the same as last time, but he got right up to the window this time - he got past the second layer.'

'Don't be silly - it was just a dream. Nobody can get past even layer one in reality,' she chuckled, as if to prove how silly the very idea was.

'How can you be so sure? Papa said when the day comes people will be so desperate, they'll do anything to survive.'

'Perhaps but that's why we have the layers in the first place. We're ready.' She picked up Emmy's trusty blankie from the armchair beside the bed and handed it to her, even though at ten years old, her sister had long grown out of childish things.

'Look Papa designed all this, remember? And he left nothing to chance. Even if anyone tried to get through layer one we'd know about it. The alarm would sound. Think about it ... if they got through the moat and thorn bushes as far as the fence and even through it, they'd still have to get past Buster and Otto. You saw what they did to the fox that came in after the chickens last time?' Cici said, reminding her of just how vicious the dogs could be.

'So even if they got to layer two, it would take them an age to get past that anyway. Papa built this house to withstand anything. The walls are five feet deep, the roof is solid concrete and the windows and doors are reinforced with steel. Even if somebody did get to the inner layer we'd already be safe below, so unless they've a couple of years to spare to wait us out, they might as well just give up anyway.'

'I don't want to be locked down there for years though ...'

Cici couldn't understand how vulnerable Emmy was when it came to her nightmares and fears about the world outside.

It was totally at odds with the confident youngster who was so capable when it came to everything else within their small confines.

'It won't ever come to that, I promise. Nobody even knows we're here, and when the time comes we'll be ready.'

Emmy nodded, glad that her big sister was always there to reassure her.

Glad for the layers of security their parents had provided so the family could survive whatever the future threw at them.

19

In the lab, Reilly was examining the backpack the journalist David Walsh had been wearing while out hiking. The grey, lightweight carrier had orange trim with a matching coloured logo marked *Inov8* in the centre. Apparently, the expensive pack was popular with speed hikers and trail runners. There was very little storage space, since most of the internal volume was given over to a water bladder with a drinking tube that led out of the top of the bag and onto a shoulder strap - where it could be unclipped for the user to bite down on the nozzle and activate the flow of liquid.

According to family and friends, the journalist had been a keen trail runner, and she wondered if his attacker had known that too.

She examined the backpack under the LED

lamp, taking a couple of hair and fibre samples before using the Wet-Vac to collect any smaller trace material.

The victim's body had been found sitting upright against a tree, an image she would remember for ever.

The ground area beneath was quite sheltered and dry with a carpet of older discarded pine needles, and she took special interest in some of the dried-on mud, which upon cursory glance seemed to have originated from a different terrain.

Further searches of the immediate area had thus far failed to pinpoint the initial attack site, and his eyeballs remained undiscovered.

Likely snatched by some hungry local foxes or badgers even.

If she could identify the primary area of assault, there would be a much better chance of finding more pertinent and useful forensic trace. Especially if there had been a struggle.

Opening the zip at the top of the backpack, she gently removed the internal bladder. There was still some liquid inside, but it started to leak out a little as she removed it. On closer inspection she could see tiny fragments embedded into the rubber, which appeared similar to what she had recovered from the canvas.

One or two of these sharp fragments seemed to have penetrated the bladder - hence the leaks - and she used a tweezers to remove a few fragments for further examination.

Then gently unscrewing the top of the bladder, she got a faint citrus whiff from within, accompanied by a less pleasant, stale scent, indicative of the fact it hadn't been opened in a while.

Reilly took a sterile syringe, and just as she was about to submerge it into the liquid in the hope of ascertaining and confirming the source of Walsh's sedation, her phone dinged nearby.

Glancing at it, she realised it was an email she'd been waiting on that could prove equally pertinent to the story of the journalist's demise.

Dear Ms Steel,

Following our discussion about the fruit samples provided, please find below a brief summation of our analysis.

Both samples are of an indigenous apple known to growers as Lady's Finger of Offaly. A dessert variety that ripens in October/November, it is known for it's sweet, greenish white flesh. The fruit matures to medium size, with a notable oblong shape that is often attributed to this particular variety - hence the name. It's an easily grown fruit suited primarily to the counties of East Leinster and parts of Southern Ulster.

We can conclude with ninety eight percent certainty that these samples derived from the same tree - ie they are genetically identical.

However, two additional findings were noted during our analysis.

One is that there is significant cell damage to the fruit, which would suggest freezing and thawing. The other finding was that the smaller immature fruits were from a different growing season to the more mature sample. Suggesting some form of fruit preservation or storage in the interim.

I've attached a copy of our laboratory results for your perusal, and please do not hesitate to contact me with any further questions.

REILLY PONDERED the missive from the Department of Agriculture. The samples, sent a couple of days before, had derived from the bigger apple found alongside Sean Shaughnessy's corpse, and the smaller ones in journalist David Walsh's eye sockets.

Two completely different and until now, apparently wholly unrelated crime scenes.

Not only had the apples originated from the same tree, but they'd been stored and perhaps even frozen in the interim - why?

The fact that they were a domestic variety and specific to a particular location could ultimately prove helpful though.

She sat back in her chair as she realised the true significance of what had just transpired.

And that the apples weren't just a symbol, but a calling card.

20

'Shite,' Kennedy spat, tossing his phone onto his over-congested desk at Harcourt Street station.

'What's up?' Chris asked.

'That callout Davis and Murphy went on earlier?' he said, linking his fingers behind his head trying to massage the rising tension away. 'Looks like it's going to be ours after all.' He clambered to his feet, lifting his jacket from the back of his chair. 'C'mon, I'll fill you in on the way.'

A little later the two detectives pulled up close to a collection of modern glass and steel apartment blocks surrounding a large granite plaza in the centre.

Once upon a time this former docklands area had been a rough impoverished part of inner city Dublin. Now it was a monument to sleek glass high-rises and modern architecture, and very much *the* place to live for affluent young professionals, following the prevalence of US tech multi-nationals setting up base nearby.

Kennedy spied the entrance to one of the newer apartment blocks, which was thick with squad cars and uniforms milling around.

Some civilians were also lingering, a few obviously just rubber-necking, while a larger group of young females about the same age as his eldest daughter, looked to be outright wailing and consoling each other.

'Can you believe this place?' he grunted, nodding at the myriad high-end cafes and restaurants with alfresco seating areas overlooking the plaza.

Where he had once cut his teeth busting street thugs and petty drug dealers, now, clean-cut, sophisticated youngsters sat beneath fancy outdoor heaters chatting over paper cups of beverages he couldn't pronounce and stroking shiny smartphones. The difference in the place struck him hard every time he came down here now.

Chris just shrugged.

He was in quare bad form these last few days, Kennedy mused. He knew he'd been keeping a close eye on Steel in the aftermath of all that ... misfortune, so maybe her being back at work so soon or something like that, had to do with his mood?

It usually did.

He then spotted their detective colleague, Sarah

Davis standing in the plaza below the relevant apartment block, and the two headed over.

'Still haven't learned to ride the bike without stabilisers, eh?' The younger detective - a slip of a thing in her mid-thirties - was good craic and Kennedy knew she'd take the ribbing in her stride.

Sarah duly rolled her eyes. 'Hilarious. You won't be cracking jokes when you see what we're up against.'

'Why are we here anyway?' Chris asked.

'All I know is Spud told me to call ye in - he's still up there. Don't even know where to begin with this one to be honest, probably best if ye just go and have a look.'

'Rightio.'

They were directed to the lifts by an officer who looked even younger than his youngest, Julie.

Upon exiting the lift on the third floor, Kennedy sniffed the air as they stepped out onto a corridor tiled in expensive-looking granite.

There looked to be six apartments on this floor, with stainless steel numbers mounted on the light grey-coloured wall beside each entrance.

They stopped at an area cordoned off at the opposite end of the corridor to the lifts, where low sunlight shone through a glazed wall framing a very nice view over the River Liffey.

Lifting the tape, he and Chris entered apartment 304, and the rotten smell that Kennedy had noticed when the lift doors opened, became even stronger.

The entryway and kitchen/living area of this place looked like it had come straight from the cover of an interior design magazine. Their other colleague Detective 'Spud' Murphy was standing with his back to them in what seemed to be a doorway through to a bedroom.

'What's the story, Spud?' he asked, announcing their arrival.

'Your guess is as good as mine,' the other man replied, standing aside to allow them full view.

Inside a bedroom with the same kind of fancy decor as all these modern swanky hotels that Kennedy could never afford, was a large king size bed, and a figure, obviously deceased, inside the covers.

Though some of the bed-coverings had been partially pulled back, presumably by the paramedics, who'd quickly realised there was nothing for them to do here.

It was times like this that Kennedy was glad years of smoking had dulled that particular sense a little, and he glanced at Chris, who was holding a hand up under his nose to avoid the worst of the stench.

'What am I actually looking at here?' he said out loud. 'Looks like this has been there for weeks ...'

'Try three days or less,' Murphy said. 'Flatmate just returned from a trip abroad to find him like ... this. When the guy left for the airport last Friday, his roomie here was in the fullest of health.'

'But what, I mean how ...' Chris trailed off. 'Are those ratchet straps?'

'I think so, he's pinned down well. Can only see from the chest up so far until M.E. gets at it, but looks as though there's a few more straps along the torso, as well as the one across his forehead.'

All three stood in silent contemplation taking in the scene. Kennedy moved closer, making sure not to contaminate anything, and manoeuvred diagonally towards the foot of the bed to get a look inside the victim's wide open mouth. Matching his eyes which seemed to stare in terror at nothingness.

'Is that it, in his mouth?' he asked.

'Yep, it's broken down a little with the heat but if you shine a torch in, you can see the little stem bit.'

'I'll take your word for it, thanks,' he said retracing his steps towards the bedroom door then studied the extension cable and several other leads trailing beneath the multiple layers of bedclothes.

'Who unplugged the cable?'

'Paramedics. The flatmate who found him just bolted - after leaving a souvenir of his own,' Murphy indicated to the floor by the wardrobe where an obvious streak of vomit could be seen but barely smelt because of the more overpowering decomposition odour.

Kennedy had seen some ugly murder scenes in his time. Most were spur of the moment, crimes of passion where stray words or unwanted actions had led to an outburst of violence. Others had been more planned but they were often the cleaner ones, a quick knife or several shots through a front door or car window.

This was ... different.

The dead guy had been bound and strapped to his own bed, wrapped in a duvet and what appeared to be an electric blanket, while also covered in layers of tinfoil - like those space blankets people at disaster scenes get draped in.

The poor divil had essentially been slow-cooked to death - with an apple shoved in his mouth for good measure, like a pig at a medieval banquet.

Roasted, even.

And the apple was obviously why he and Chris been called in for this.

In true form, Steel was already ahead of the game and had since filled them in on the Dept of Agriculture's recent findings.

If this apple happened to also come from the same source, they were in business.

Or in trouble, depending on how you looked at it.

THE THREE DETECTIVES retreated downstairs once the M.E. arrived, and as they exited the building, all were once again taken aback at the marked increase in the crowd now gathered in the immediate vicinity.

The police cordon had been pushed further and wider across the plaza, with several officers holding the line while fending off questions from rubberneckers and increasingly agitated fellow residents momentarily prevented from entering.

Sarah headed over to join them.

'Where did this shower come from?' her partner asked, referring to the crowds, the majority with iPhone devices up and pointed at them, recording proceedings for posterity.

'Turns out the victim's a bit of a celeb. Will Vines, prolific YouTuber and Tiktokker?' Sarah told him.

'Come again? In English this time,' Kennedy grumbled, eyebrows raised.

'OK Pops, I'll rephrase it. He was super-famous and much beloved by Millennials.'

'Yeah I get that much; I've two meself at home. And I know what YouTube is - for looking at old football matches and stuff. But what in the name of all things holy is a Tiktokker?'

'The latest social media craze. This fella isn't small fry either - he's a proper star, raking it in with high-end lifestyle sponsorships; travel deals, designer label endorsements, you name it.'

'There's proper money in all that shite?' Kennedy looked perplexed.

'Remind me to give you a crash course in modern culture sometime,' Sarah drawled. Then she made a face. 'But without wanting to speak ill of the dead, I'd be no fan of the guy, let me tell you.'

'Meself and modern culture are on a need to know basis, thanks very much. But would you look at this place, three o'clock in the afternoon on a weekday - why aren't these kids in school, or in their jobs or wherever? Or is it just us Boomers who actually do a day's work anymore...' he added, utilising terminology he'd picked up from his girls in an attempt to persuade the younger detective that he wasn't a complete dinosaur altogether.

The Boomer thing was Selena and Julie's current moniker for their long-suffering dad.

He looked again at the crowd of youngsters gathered in the plaza, wailing like people used to at the Beatles back in the day. Fair enough, since the Fab Four were huge stars, world-renowned musicians, *proper* famous.

Whereas your man inside? Kennedy shook his head.

Maybe he needed a crash course on this palaver after all.

21

Reilly waited for the M.E. to finish up before letting the team loose in the influencer's apartment - all the while wondering how much a place like this cost.

The notion wasn't purely academic either; thanks to a recent missive from her landlord declaring that he intended on selling the Ranelagh property and was thus giving her notice to vacate.

Having lived in the compact and well-located flat since first arriving in the city almost four years ago, the idea of having to wade back into a rapidly inflationary Dublin rental market was not one she relished.

But she knew for sure she wouldn't be able to afford somewhere like this, which she guessed in this area rented for a couple of grand a month.

Nice work if you could get it...

Lucy and Gary would go through the plush

apartment with a fine tooth comb, not just for trace related to this incident, but also from another equally important perspective - any further potential crossover from the other crime scenes, given the apple connection.

The apartment block common areas looked immaculately maintained, so they were lucky on that score not to have to trawl through the nightmare of cataloguing and crossmatching trace from multiple residents so as to rule them out.

She hadn't yet seen the body (or latest apple insertion) but had been given a heads-up on what to expect.

Reilly headed up the stairwell that ascended a half floor at a time, before it returned on itself and rose to the second half floor.

On each level thanks to the glazed wall, she had a clear view down to the plaza area in front of the building.

Just as she reached the final ascent, she looked out the window and paused. The crowd seemed to be growing fast, at least two or three hundred people out there now, she figured.

Whoever was behind these murders - all deeply theatrical in nature (and given the evidence commonality, they now needed to work on the assumption that it was the same person) it seemed that causing death wasn't enough - torture also played a significant element.

The doer also took a lot of time and imagination

over the set-up, seemed to relish the means as much as the result.

Something that her FBI mentor Daniel Forrest, used to say about exhibitionist murderers came back to her.

'Pride is often their Achilles heel, because their need for admiration is just as strong as the urge to kill.'

This kind of killer often stayed close by to watch once their grisly tableau was discovered - talking to onlookers, listening to rumours - so as to draw out and even heighten their gratification.

She looked again at the crowd as they stood vigil; the majority holding up devices and taking pictures and videos - mostly of themselves as they cried - as if publicly trying to outdo one another with their grief.

Modern life was weird sometimes.

But if this killer was an exhibitionist, then perhaps they too would employ a smartphone in amongst the crowd, savouring the impact of their work and even recording it for posterity?

She pulled her phone from her pocket and called Chris's number.

'What's up?'

'Guessing there are security cameras in this building?'

'Yeah, in the lobby, the lifts and more on each landing at the access points. We're already on it.'

'What about exterior CCTV? I'm just looking out the window at that crowd behind you. Any way we could get some good quality footage of the

Looky-loos out there? In case our perp is a bit of a voyeur.'

'Not a bad idea. I'll check.'

She nodded and was about to hang up, when a newly arriving vehicle - a white van - caught her attention.

'What about that TV truck? They can take footage from an elevated position, not to mention better resolution too.'

All the better for zooming in on anything shady afterward.

If the doer was a showman, they surely wouldn't want to miss this circus.

22

Hanging up, Chris duly approached the TV2 broadcasting crew, who were setting up just outside the cordon, and headed straight to the attractive female reporter Grainne O'Toole, who he'd occasionally come across in person, but had seen onscreen many times more.

Several people stood around recording the crew with their devices. The public's increasing compulsion to film bloody everything and anything these days was both a blessing and a curse.

Yes, they'd had many a breakthrough using smartphone footage and dashboard cameras. But on the flip-side, it attracted way bigger crowds to emergency situations. The irony of the fact that so many right now were holding up devices with miniature apples emblazoned across the back of them wasn't lost on Chris either.

He spoke briefly with Grainne and her colleagues and the camera guy agreed to his request for some high quality footage of the crowd from an elevated vantage point.

Unfortunately the quid pro quo was a two minute piece to camera from him, but he knew he could just trot out the usual spiel while saying nothing. He just hated going on camera.

He headed back over in Kennedy's direction. 'Will they do it?' he asked.

'Yep, they're going to shoot from over there,' Chris pointed to the second-floor balcony of a high end restaurant nearby. 'I'm going to scan the crowd too when they start rolling. See if there's any reaction.'

'Why don't I go back up and keep an eye from the building, and you stay here on the phone to me. I can give you the heads-up if anyone blinks.'

'Good idea.'

Kennedy made his way back inside the apartment block, while the cameraman positioned his tripod on the restaurant balcony, having got the OK from management.

As his partner stood in place behind the glazed wall overlooking the plaza, Chris gave the TV guy the thumbs up and he slowly turned the camera towards the crowd.

After a minute or two, Chris spoke into the handset. 'Anything?'

'Not so far, most of those eejits are all still too busy filming themselves bawling. See all the flowers? You'd swear yer man was John Lennon.'

Kennedy was referring to several bunches of flowers laid just outside the police cordon that did indeed put Chris in mind of the infamous shooting in New York.

A couple of minutes later, his partner spoke again; his tone a little more urgent this time. 'Hold on a sec, there's a fella a way back close to the canal there - see the No Swimming sign? Black hoodie with red writing on it. He just pulled his hood up and started backing up when a few others spotted the TV camera. Looks to be on his own too.'

Chris scanned the crowd from below. He knew exactly where the sign was; living nearby he'd spent a lot of time down in this very spot every summer, enjoying a coffee and watching local youths blatantly ignore the swimming restrictions and splashing into the canal directly from the plaza. The actual dock for which this area was named, was a rectangular body of water fed on one side by the river and the canal on the other.

Where once it was used by barges to transport goods inland, now the canal was purely for leisure pursuits - especially in warmer weather.

Chris ducked under the police tape and waded deftly through the crowd. He picked up the pace as he headed to the signpost, recalling that the boardwalk area alongside it led to three possible exit points from the plaza itself.

'Talk to me.'

'Sorry, thought I'd lost him for a sec. He's turned in the other direction now, away from the crowd towards the pedestrian bridge at the far right hand side. Beside that place with the big round yellow sign ... Poco Loco, I think it says?'

'I know the one.' He quickened his pace even more.

'That's it. Once you pass through that area you'll see him towards the edge of the plaza hurrying away. Small blue backpack over his shoulder, couldn't see that before now.'

Chris cleared the crowd and saw their person of interest walking more briskly now. The guy was too far away to call out to him to stop, so he broke into a gentle jog.

Once he'd gained a bit more ground, the guy looked over his shoulder and promptly broke into a run, heading straight for the pedestrian bridge that led to a busy cross street.

'Feck, he's on the move,' Kennedy spat.

'Yep, I've eyes on. Get a couple of squads out.' Chris slipped his phone into his trousers pocket and broke into a run.

He could see his target crossing the bridge and turning right, and had to shout at a group of kids walking four abreast blocking his way.

As he crossed the bridge and rounded the corner,

he saw the suspect unlocking a bike attached to the railings of an older building. In a single movement he'd released the bike allowing the lock to fall to the ground and hopped on, pushing himself off with his feet as he started to pedal down the path and then dismounted the kerb to join the main body of traffic.

Damn...

Realising his foot pursuit was now done for, Chris pulled out the phone again and put a call in with a description of the guy and requesting as many bodies on the street as possible, all the while trying to get his breath back.

He was getting too old for this shit...

Approaching the railings to which the bike had been attached, he stood over the discarded lock, while an onlooker stared at him in turn from the doorway of a nearby hairdressing salon.

'You OK, love?' the woman asked in a thick inner-city accent.

'Detective,' he panted, flashing his ID between gulps of air.

'Scumbags are gone very brazen around here lately. Selling gear right outside the school 'an all. Fair play to you for putting the shits up them; they have the run of the place.'

Chris smiled tightly. 'Did you get a good look at him?'

'Not really, sure they all go round with their hoods up. Shouldn't be allowed.'

'Can I give you my card, maybe if you do see the guy again or recognise him you could let me know.'

'No bother.'

'One more thing,' he said, his gaze on the discarded bike lock. 'I don't suppose you could spare me plastic bag ...'

23

Chris then headed back across the bridge and around the still-crowded plaza where he spotted Kennedy talking to the TV crew.

'Any joy?' his partner asked.

'No - he took off on a pedal bike, station has three squads out and they've put all units on notice.'

'Eh ... can I ask why you've a pink shower cap in your hand?'

'He dropped the bike lock outside a hairdressers,' Chris told him. 'I won't ask how you knew it was a shower cap.'

'Teenage daughters bud, I'm wading through that kinda stuff in my gaff.'

'So, you were chatting to the camera guy - reckon he got anything?'

'Says he did a good slow pan of the crowd, and then you tearing off after yer man.'

'Great. Hopefully somebody picks him up in the meantime anyway.'

'You want to go for a spin around, see if we can spot him?'

Chris shook his head. 'Little point I think - he could be anywhere by now. Besides there's enough to be dealing with here.' He glanced back at the ever-burgeoning crowd and the lit candles which had since joined the growing pile of floral tributes. A proper vigil. 'How does word get out so soon?'

'Sure the kids are all practically wired up to each other these days, can't shit for the world knowing,' Kennedy sniffed. 'According to Spud, the flatmate - the very same fella who found him, mind you - feckin' posted about it on his social media after the paramedics arrived. Did you ever in all your life ...'

Chris raised an eyebrow. 'Obviously got over his sick stomach quick enough then.'

'I'm only surprised he didn't snap a picture and post that up too for likes and hearts, or whatever it is they're all addicted to getting. At least he had the cop on not to do that.'

'That we know of...' Chris murmured.

'Think it's time we went and had a bit of a chat with him altogether. He's with one of the local guys in a place a few streets down. Seems that fella's 'famous' too, so they had to take him somewhere quieter there was so many kids swarming over him.'

'Great. But assuming Vines is the same guy I'm thinking of, then he's fairly well-known for something else too.' When Kennedy looked blank, he added. 'The name didn't mean anything to you?'

'Seriously, what makes you think I'd have the first feckin' notion ...?'

Then just behind, Chris spied Grainne beckoning him over, evidently looking for him to deliver on his part of the bargain. He paused, realising the last thing he should do while in earshot of media was fill Kennedy in on Vines' more ... controversial real-world profile. He'd also need to try and dissuade Grainne from making any such leaps as it was.

'You carry on and I'll meet you there,' he told him, 'I need to get this over and done with.'

His partner threw an eye at the bike lock. 'Better get rid of that too, before you're ready for your close-up.'

TEMPORARILY SIDESTEPPING the TV journalist and her crew by professing important police business, Chris headed back into the apartment building, going upstairs to see intermittent camera flashes emitting from inside and illuminating the hallway as it grew darker in the fading evening light.

Nodding at the officer on guard duty, he peered in the door to see three GFU figures in various stages of collecting evidence.

'A moment?' he called to Reilly, stepping away from the doorway as the scent of decay still lingered.

'How'd it go?' she asked, placing her mask high on her forehead.

'You were right about the crowd. We got a runner.'

'You have someone in custody?'

'Not yet, he took off pretty quick. But hopefully the footage will give us something more concrete. I do have this, though.' He held up the bike lock wrapped in the pink plastic, as she looked on, bemused. 'Bike lock - he dropped it when he took off.'

'Definitely a he, then?'

'I didn't get close enough to see for sure, but I'd imagine so. Took off on the bike towards the city centre. Squads are on the lookout so you never know.'

Reilly took the lock and had a look inside. 'Good find, thanks.'

Despite himself he couldn't help but bask in the light of her praise.

'How's all going here?'

She shook her head. 'To paraphrase, I think we're gonna need a bigger lab. Between this and the other two there's a tonne to get through now.'

'I don't envy you. We're about to interview the flatmate, seems he's responsible for the fan club. All over social media long before the family was even notified.'

'O'Brien'll be thrilled about that.'

'Yup.'

'I didn't get a chance to speak to the other detectives, but how come you two were called in for this - was it the apple?'

Chris met her gaze. Clearly she hadn't made any connection either.

'Not exactly. Seems these three men have more in common than meets the eye.'

24

'You're listening to 'Drive It Home' on FM102 this fine evening, and today we're joined by regular contributors Suzi Cox and Derek Hayes to discuss the recent erm ... shocking ... crime wave happening across our fair city. Evening folks'

'Evening Dave, interesting choice of words.'

'I know, forgive me ... but a killing spate targeting some well-known figures - should the residents of our capital be worried, Derek?'

'Maybe. To be fair, I'm guilty of being a bit ... ambivalent when I hear about gangland murders and the like but ...'

'I agree with Derek, by now we're all almost immune to news of gangland-related tit for tat stuff, and the majority don't really care. Scumbags killing scumbags. Even though communities are being terrorised and the streets we're living on are being turned into war zones. It angers me.'

'Derek, Suzi makes a good point. No matter how ambivalent we feel about gangland turf-wear targets, surely the real victims are the innocent citizens living those communities?'

'Agreed but I feel this is a whole different discussion. We all know we're not comparing like with like here. The latest victims can only be described as regular citizens.'

'Regular citizens ... seriously? For starters, one is a fellow media colleague, another famously acted as legal counsel for the other, a prominent social media star who shall not be named, but we all know who we're talking about here, don't we?'

'Yes, but that's as far as it goes...no naming names please, Suzi.'

'I agree to a point, but obviously something like this is going to naturally attract a lot more attention. From the police included.'

'So just because some celeb - and I use that term lightly - is the target, more resources should automatically be employed to catch those responsible? Frankly, I'm amazed by the coverage and media attention given to the other victims already - all men incidentally. And if we're in agreement that gangland targets are often of questionable character, I think we could certainly be forgiven for asking the same question of this particular group too.'

'If I'm understanding you correctly - you're questioning the character of these recent victims, Suzi?'

'Your words, Dave, not mine. We all knew of these men professionally, and my personal belief is that some of David Walsh's work in particular did a lot of damage in *that high-profile legal situation we're all familiar with, and which connects them all. You don't need to be a genius to work that one out.'*

'OK, Suzi, dangerous ground here and I'm really not sure we should even speculate... better leave that one there, before my producer keels over!

Up next on the show - are cyclists the city's transport saviour - or scourge? We'll be hearing from taxi drivers after the break.'

25

Chris joined Kennedy and Will Vines' flatmate in a cafe not far from where his potential suspect had scarpered.

He still felt edgy after giving chase, and didn't feel up to the more pedestrian tasks of conducting interviews.

He was also keen to get a look at the accompanying footage from the news crew, but they were disinclined to hand it over until he'd given them a scoop.

But Chris wasn't prepared to make any statements just yet, not until he'd had a chance to discuss all permutations with Kennedy.

In fact, it may well be a good thing that his partner remained non-the-wiser about Vines; it meant that at least one of them would be coming at this interview (and the entire investigation) with a fresh eye, free of any related baggage.

The front area was busy with customers, but he could see a small sitting area of two long couches facing each other with a low coffee table in between. Several chairs had been lined up to stop other patrons occupying tables nearby, while a uniformed officer stood sentry in front of the area.

Chris headed to where Kennedy and the flatmate were sitting opposite each other. He looked at the pale-skinned, floppy haired kid, who looked to be in his early twenties, his skinny arms and hands cradling an oversized cup of coffee, and decided to sit next to him to psych him out a little - still cheesed off at him for spreading the news of his so-called friend's demise far and wide before the family had even been notified.

And worse, potentially triggering a media speculation frenzy.

Plus, with no signs of breaking and entering, anyone with access to the apartment was a potential suspect.

'And here he is, my partner Detective Delaney,' Kennedy offered by way of introduction. 'Greg here has been filling me in on how today unfolded.'

Chris nodded a curt greeting. 'Sorry about your friend, not a nice sight to come home to from a holiday.'

'Oh, Will wasn't my friend - we just lived together. And I was actually coming back from a business trip. Hashtag guyboss.'

What the ...? Chris was taken aback by the kid's

flat, emotionless tone, almost as if he was bored by it all.

And what the hell was this hashtag bullshit?

'A shock nonetheless?' he urged, trying to read the little prick, who seemed more interested in his phone notifications pinging away on the table.

'Sure ...'

'Business trip ... what do you do for a living, Greg?' Kennedy asked then.

'I'm an influencer.' Then he sighed as they waited for him to explain further. 'I partner with various high level brands to introduce their products to my audience?'

'Rightio. Same as your flatmate?'

'Emm not really, Will was more into vlogs and Tiktok. I'm more old school. Insta mostly.'

Chris clocked Kennedy's expression and could almost read his mind. Old school indeed... he knew he'd be hearing about that one later with a few choice words thrown in for good measure.

And he couldn't blame him.

'OK, but a similar line of work then. Do you know of anybody that would've had any issues with Will?' Kennedy asked, completely oblivious.

'I don't think so - apart from the obvious.' Another eye roll. 'There's never any shortage of jealously and bitter trolls, but nothing serious as far as I'm aware. Not lately anyway.'

'We spoke with the management company; you and William were joint owners of the property?'

'Yes, we bought it together a few years ago.'

'Forgive me, I'm just a little confused,' Chris put in then. 'You said you and Will Vines weren't friends, yet you purchased an expensive apartment together?'

'I didn't say we weren't friendly. When we bought the apartment we were a couple - engaged actually.'

At this, Kennedy raised an eyebrow and quickly followed up. 'Right. But you said you are no longer 'friends' so I take it you're no longer engaged either?'

The conversation was so surreal, in any other circumstances it would've been humorous, Chris thought. But there was nothing funny about Vines' death.

'Correct. So sad ... we just drifted apart. We'd put the apartment on the market, but would've had to pay too much off the mortgage to sell because we'd overpaid for it at the time. Neither of us could afford that, so we decided to wait a couple more years for the market to recover.'

These guys were superstars in their field, supposedly loaded, and yet they couldn't afford to pay off the remaining mortgage balance? Something wasn't adding up here...

Hashtag dodgyAF.

'Must've been awkward. Living with a former fiancé.'

'Not really. We just moved on with our own lives. I know he was seeing a girl from Poland for a while, not sure if they're still an item and I don't have any contact for her either before you ask.'

'A girl?' Kennedy clarified, frowning.

Greg exhaled heavily and rolled his eyes. 'Yes, a girl, Detective. Everyone knows Will is ... *was* fluid.'

'Sorry, wha ...?' The big man was a step away from needing a translator.

'Actually, he's a flipper, used to like boys, now likes girls,' Greg continued, matter of factly. 'Unfortunately for him.'

'Right. Flipper. That's a new one on me I have to say.'

Chris scrolled through his phone while Kennedy took the lead. Not because he was bored, but to try and get a better handle on these two and why they attracted so much adoration, when it was obvious they were both pricks.

For Greg, the search had quickly thrown up reams of social media links and various other online mentions, but a recent tweet in particular caught his eye.

'The world is a lonelier, sadder place today. Farewell @ItsWillyV - may your beautiful soul rest in peace.'

'Greg, can I ask you what you did upon discovering your flatmate and former fiancé in that state earlier?'

Another prolonged eye roll. 'Duh ... keep up Detective. I've already been through this.'

Cheeky little so-and-so...He'd had just about enough of this twerp.

'Now listen here ...' Kennedy growled, but Chris cut him off.

'Fine, I know what you did. You called 999 and sent out a bloody tweet about your ex fiancé's death. The thing I haven't yet figured out is which came first.'

'Does it matter? It's not as though the cavalry could do anything anyway. And Will's audience deserved to know. He was so adored by everyone.' Greg sniffed and wiped a crocodile tear from one eye.

'Yeah I'm sure his parents and loved ones were thrilled to hear about it from social media. Thousands of compete strangers notified before your *friend* had been officially identified. And I think we both know Will wasn't adored by everyone ...' he added meaningfully.

The flatmate didn't react, his attention already distracted by a smaller crowd now gathering outside the cafe window - again with their phones to the ready. And then, as if he'd suddenly been struck by a serious case of remorse, Greg began to weep openly.

To borrow one of Kennedy's phrases; *For football's sake* ...

Didn't this despicable little twerp have any moral self awareness at all - or had he sacrificed it all to the Insta-gods?

It was actually sickening.

'Look Greg, have you someplace else to stay for a bit?' Kennedy asked, evidently bamboozled by the theatrics. 'With family maybe? The apartment will be off limits for a while.'

'Oh my God I'm *never* going back there. Gonna crash at my sister's place probably.'

'And where might that be? Just in case of any follow up questions.'

'In Blackrock.'

'Grand, we'll arrange a lift for you. Wait here and we'll send somebody to get you. We may need to call on you again over the coming days, so sit tight.'

'Of course. I can't thank you enough detectives.' His entire demeanour - personality even, had changed utterly with the appearance of spectators. Like an actor on stage playing to an audience. 'Just promise me you'll find out who did this?' he pleaded. 'Will deserves justice.'

'WHAT DID you make of all that?' Chris asked, when they left the self-proclaimed social media star in the care of one of the local uniforms.

'I think I feel old.'

'Slimy little fecker. Completely unaffected by the loss of someone he was close to, until those kids outside started to gather. Then it was all Wailing Wall of Jerusalem.'

'Yeah, I know what you mean. Like he was playing a part.'

'That's exactly it, playing to an audience - a projection of how he wanted to be seen by the public. Didn't seem to give a shite about us, or Vines for that matter. He deserves justice, my arse.'

'On any other occasion, I'd have him as my first name on the suspect list, but ... nah, seems like more of a keyboard warrior to me,' Kennedy sniffed. 'God be with the days when if you had a beef with someone, you came right out and said it to their face.'

'We'll look into Greg's timeline and alibi, but I suspect we'd be barking up the wrong tree.' Chris took a deep breath, figuring it was time to break it to him. 'To be honest, when it comes to Will Vines, there's a hell of a lot more to contend with.'

26

Lina looked up from her book and saw her two daughters also reading quietly by the open fire.

Outside, strong gusts of winds drove heavy sleety rain against the windows. She felt safe, warm and cozy in here; just her and her girls.

She had her doubts about the choices she'd made for them sometimes and whenever that happened Peter had aways been her rock, the one she'd always turned to for reassurance.

But all that started to change when the first signs of weakness appeared. Looking back now, she could see the progression all too clearly.

He would be mid-flow in conversation and suddenly lose his train of thought. While at first they would laugh, he soon became frustrated, then gradually more and more withdrawn until at last deeply paranoid that the end had started. It was as if a war was already raging in his head and the only thing that seemed to calm him was the alcohol.

The first time he struck her was a shock.

Lina had returned from getting supplies, and he had accused her of taking too long, demanded to know who she was talking to, calling her vile names she'd never heard him utter before.

His bouts of anger and rage gradually increased, and all too soon she found herself trying to placate and defuse.

Ironic that the safe space the two had created for their daughters was being threatened by what they'd both sworn to protect them from.

Lina had never come to the point of deciding that they would be better off without him though.

Even after each attack, even after he had become more physical with the girls, she still loved him.

After all, the two were becoming more unruly with age - Emmy in particular -and needed discipline if they were to survive in the world after The Correction.

Lina continued loving Peter even when she struck with the fire poker the fatal blow that he would never wake up from. And plunged the knife in his back thereafter just to be sure.

After that, she had wondered if she could realistically continue to raise the girls on her own.

To keep them away from the cancerous society that lay beyond their retreat. Yet, she knew she must.

She looked at them now reading, learning about

the world. The beauty and wonder of nature and animals, and the ultimate flaw that was Man.

They were both in their early teens now, and growing up fast - and the lack of modern day distractions meant they were thriving intellectually.

Occasionally she worried that the lack of social interaction would leave them incapable when they would need to dip into the outside world. And so they introduced role play and practiced for multiple scenarios. Lina also had them drilled on what they needed to do if anything happened to her.

Soon she'd start bringing them with her on some supply runs to test out certain scenarios in the real world.

Just in case.

'Mama, what does this word mean?' Cici asked, rising to her feet and walking across to where her mother sat.

'Umm,' Lina paused, mentally choosing her words as she glanced at pages depicting black and white images of holes in the ground filled with the limbs of the slaughtered. 'Genocide is the mass killing of a large group of people from a particular ethnic background.'

'Looks horrible, why would anybody do that?

'Unfortunately sweetheart, one half of humankind is born with a cruel ... sickness. Born with the power to love and be loved, to do great things and terrible things.'

'Is that what the Correction will look like?' Cici's eyes looked sad, with more than a hint of fear.

Lina took the book from her and set it on the table.

'Not quite. Anyhow, in here is no need for you to worry. We are completely safe, just us girls.'

Still, as she looked at her eldest's face she could still see the questions rolling around inside her mind.

'Was Papa part of the ... sickness?'

'Unfortunately, yes.'

She nodded and looked again at the book. 'Then I'm so glad we're not men.'

27

Chris parked the car in the first available slot, not caring if he was straight or between the lines. He had stuck to the script and not given anything away on the news.

Not that it made much of a difference anyway.

He knew it would only be a matter of time before the media picked up on the connection between the victims and jumped to the obvious conclusion.

At least they didn't know anything about the apples thing.

Yet.

He was nearly out of the car before the engine had shut down, feeling that same old adrenaline surge he'd been experiencing so rarely lately.

In his hand was a memory stick with footage from TV2, and the management company were also sending over CCTV from inside the building covering the relevant time frame.

He was confident that if they could make some headway in ID-ing that suspect, they were onto something.

'Davis and Murphy back yet do you know?' he asked Kennedy who was struggling to keep up alongside him.

In more ways than one. The big man had been completely blindsided by the Will Vines thing and had needed his memory refreshed.

'Yeah, think they've finished up a door-to-door with the residents,' he replied.

'Lets get them in to review the footage, and then we can all compare notes and make a plan of action for tomorrow.'

'We've got Shock's ex to chat to in the morning, don't forget.'

Chris cursed inwardly. They really were going to have to become expert jugglers. Three concurrent and connected murders; the caseload would be massive - even with the other two detectives supporting.

First, he went to check if anybody matching the description of the runner had since been taken into custody, disappointed but not surprised to learn that no one had been apprehended.

Then they walked through the open plan offices in the police station and headed directly for the meeting room, where the audiovisual equipment was located.

'I'll give the other two a shout,' Kennedy said as he peeled away towards Murphy's desk.

'And grab one of the tech lads too.'

Chris flicked on the lights before heading over to a desktop computer linked to a projector. Taking out the storage device marked with the TV2 logo he woke the screen and inserted the device into place, selecting the correct options from the menu as they popped up.

Kennedy returned, followed by Sarah Davis and Spud Murphy, who carried a large brown folder under his arm.

'Heard you were a bit slow off the mark earlier?' the younger cop teased and Chris looked up unimpressed.

'Hilarious. Hope you've been doing more than scratching your arse since?'

'You'll be glad to hear we have most of the neighbours canvassed,' Murphy said laying the folder on a table and sitting down.

'Most, what did you do with the rest of the day?'

'Court duty I'm afraid. Case resumed in the afternoon, that's going to take up a lot of our time till it adjourns,' Sarah said apologetically.

'Timing is shit, but what else is new. Anything from the neighbours?' Kennedy asked.

'Well yes, as it happens. The couple in 301 at the end of the corridor. Been there since the building first opened. Had some interesting observations on the two boys. Did you know they were engaged?'

Murphy announced with some drama as though making a huge revelation.

'Yeah, spoke to the flatmate. Verifying his account of the timeline with flight records etc as we speak. Anything else?'

'Did you also know...' Murphy continued, undeterred that his first revelation had fallen flat, 'that in the early days of taking up residence, there were multiple complaints made about excess noise and that the Odd Couple were prone to drunken arguments?'

'I'm not sure that's kosher these days,' Chris pointed out. 'The Odd Couple thing.'

'Downright homophobic actually,' Sarah agreed.

'Ah sure ye know I don't mean any harm...' Murphy shook his head.

'Anyway,' his partner said, moving on. 'There were several noise complaints, four of which resulted in a squad car being sent out. No charges brought though. The management company also issued two separate written warnings about antisocial behaviour to the occupants of 304.'

'Yer man I spoke to about the CCTV didn't mention that,' Kennedy grumbled.

'This is all going back three years or more, everything seems to have been quiet since then.'

'Would tally with what the flatmate said about them splitting up and continuing to live together.'

'Weird if they were at each other's throats,'

Murphy made a face. 'But this whole bloody setup is weird anyway. Or am I allowed say that?' he drawled.

Chris couldn't disagree with that one. 'Let's just wait until we've verified Greg's alibi and the pathologist comes back with a time of death - which could be tricky given the circumstances,' he pointed out, as a member of the tech team appeared.

They duly dimmed the lights and Chris took up a position alongside him. 'Roll it there, Alan.'

The TV2 footage opened with an exterior shot panning across the plaza and over the crowd.

'OK, hold it there.' He then moved to the projected image on the wall. 'Keep an eye on this guy in front of the sign.'

The footage continued to play, and the highlighted individual could be seen pulling up his hood and turning around.

At this point Chris could see himself making his way along the front of the crowd before moving through them at the sign post and the suspect correspondingly picking up the pace as he looked over his shoulder and bolted towards the footbridge at the top of the shot.

'Can you rewind and zoom in on the suspect?' he directed, before turning to the others. 'There's a chance that our doer might be the kind to admire his own handiwork,' he explained, echoing Reilly's words and feeling a little odd that she wasn't here to review all this.

It was the kind of thing she wouldn't have missed for the world before.

He shook the thoughts from his head when the tech guy gave him the thumbs up and replayed the required zoomed-in shot.

Image was a little grainy, but as the short section played on a loop, it seemed there was a good chance they'd be able to pull a decent quality still - hopefully enough to identify their runner.

But next they needed to discuss the elephant in the room.

'OK, I'm sure we've all figured out by now that Vines was the defendant in that big High Court assault case last year, with Sean Shaughnessy acting as his legal counsel. The question is, does David Walsh's writing about the controversy fit into all of this too?

And if so, then obviously we need to talk to the Joyce family.'

28

The following morning, Chris pulled into the window of the McDonald's drive-through closest to his place.

The habit on the way to work had started as a convenient way to grab a coffee without having to park up, then it turned into a 'sure I might as well grab some food since there's nothing in the fridge' excuse and gone from there.

He pressed the button to lower the driver's side window, and gave his order before moving on to the collection point.

Placing the coffee in the centre console drinks holder he put the open bag of food on the seat between his legs and headed for the station, munching as he made his way through the relatively light early morning traffic.

He knew he'd been far too slow off the mark

yesterday chasing that lad, thanks in no small part to bad habits like this. If he didn't cop himself on he'd be worse than Kennedy soon.

Another reason to change things up.

He'd been trying to get a suitable opportunity to have a chat with his partner about the promotion prospect, but the right time just never seemed to arise - especially now when they were so inundated.

He could receive a confirmation letter or phone call any day, so he needed to make time before somebody higher in the chain let it slip.

Especially when he had a fair idea what his partner's reaction would be.

There was a time when being off the streets and office-bound would never have appealed to Chris either, but this opportunity was a chance to move up through the ranks and make a difference at a higher level.

He badly needed a change, and the thought of more regular hours and a dependable social life was beginning to appeal more and more.

He needed to plot a life course with more focus on things that could bring him fulfilment - though the question was whether the highly political world of Garda senior management was conducive to that.

Reaching the station, Chris pulled into his designated parking space and switched off the engine, taking the stairs up to the office instead of the lift, in leu of any other exercise he'd be getting today.

. . .

'You're in early,' he greeted, spotting Kennedy already at his desk.

'Yeah, said I might as well make a start before we head out to see Shaughnessy's wife. I was only lying in bed thinking about it all anyway.'

'Same here.'

Kennedy flicked through some sheets of paper on his desk and turned one for Chris to see.

'What's that?'

'The 'fan mail' Shaughnessy's secretary spoke about. Some pretty nasty stuff. No direct threats or anything so far, just a lot of 'Burn in Hell Scumbag' type sentiment. Here have a read of this.'

'I don't know how you can sleep at night you piece of shit. My son is dead and the man responsible is walking around free because of you. That makes you as guilty as him. When it happens again to somebody else's kid it will be on you. I hope and pray there is a special place in hell for people like you.'

'Nice,' Chris said. 'I suppose you can't be in his game without making a few enemies, especially with who his friends are.'

'Plenty of people he had dealings with are more than capable of murder; I just don't see any of them having the panache to use the methods we've seen.'

Chris finished his coffee, grinning at Kennedy's use of 'panache' and wondering where he'd picked that one up. 'What do you think about this whole Vines connection and the court case?' he asked.

'Sarah's going back through the transcripts at the minute, see if anything jumps out. Probably an idea to speak to the Joyce girl herself too,' he mused, as their aforementioned colleague walked towards them, her eyes bleary following an all-nighter.

'You definitely don't remember the trial in question Pops,' Sarah said, making a face. 'The accuser, Linda Joyce took her own life shortly after the not-guilty judgement?'

'Jesus.'

'Yup. Mayhem. Especially when publicly there were two definite camps when it came to our defendant. Will Vines' adoring minions were very quick to support him, accusing Linda Joyce of fabricating the charge and trying to ride on his coattails. Whereas others thought he was your classic male celeb predator.'

'Celeb my arse,' Kennedy harrumphed.

'Maybe not so much amongst our generation,' Sarah said charitably, given she was a good fifteen years younger and thus more au fait with who's-who in modern Irish culture. 'But you saw them all yourself yesterday.'

'What about the family then?' Chris asked. Linda Joyce's grieving family would be obvious route for anyone with a grudge against their daughter's attacker, or indeed his solicitor.

'Mother and father still alive and together. Linda was the only girl - two older brothers,' Sarah confirmed.

Kennedy re-read another piece of Sean Shaughnessy's 'fan-mail' before sliding it across the table for the others to see.

'A chat with the brothers will indeed be in order.'

29

Reilly picked up the court-stamped folder Sarah Davis had couriered over, and sat back in her office chair - needing to familiarise herself with the legal proceedings involving all three victims which now appeared to be at the very heart of the current investigation.

The sexual assault case in question had taken place last year over a four week span, and the complainant Linda Joyce had delivered some of her evidence through video-link.

The accused, popular social media influencer William Vines had an impressive legal team - headed up of course, by the now infamous Sean Shaughnessy.

The evidence in the case was scant at best - witness testimony in relation to a social event leading up to the alleged assault, as well as some physical evidence in the form of the girl's clothing, plus some WhatsApp messages and social media posts giving a little context to the night in question.

Reilly knew better than most the importance of evidence to secure a win, and while there was no doubting Ms Joyce's strength of convictions, unfortunately that was often not enough.

As she continued to read through the transcripts, one thing that very quickly became evident was the level of mainstream and social media interest in the case.

The judge had firmly directed the jury to stay away from both media on several occasions, given the defendant's high profile, and equally high level of media interest. As well as taken the unusual step of pleading with anyone present in the court to be extra-vigilant in their related commentary so as not to risk a collapsed case.

She scanned quickly through two days's worth of testimony and questioning of the plaintiff.

Shaughnessy's line of questioning had been focused on Linda Joyce's previous knowledge and interactions with the defendant.

The girl recounted events concerning a particular Irish company for which Vines was a brand ambassador.

Reilly typed in an online search for Vines plus the relevant brand name, and scrolled through the results page.

Several Instagram and TikTok posts detailed a

smiling Vines pictured in various Dublin nighttime hotspots, champagne or cocktail glass in hand.

She clicked on another video clip of him, this time in a car showroom introducing an expensive sports car that scant few of his followers could afford.

This guy was posing as a film or sports star while his followers lived vicariously through him, lapping up the glamorous lifestyle he projected.

Will Vines' handsome smile and obvious charisma aside, Reilly wondered what it was about this guy, over the hordes of others trying to set themselves up as influencers, that made him successful.

That all-important X-factor, she supposed. But was it the case that Vines had what it took, or just took what he wanted?

Sean Shaughnessy had been very specific in his questioning about Linda Joyce's own aspirations in trying to gain a social media following in order to tap in to the increasingly lucrative influencer 'market'.

He painted a picture of Linda as some sort of hanger-on groupie trying to latch onto Vines coat-tails to increase her own profile.

And a considerable amount of time querying her about the infamous night of the accusation - the launch of a brand new city nightclub and bar, where the two had been pictured and recorded 'cuddling' as Shaughnessy put it.

The night that Linda had claimed William Vines had forcibly raped her after she'd gone back to his apartment in the docklands area.

The defence team claimed that Linda had sought Vines out for attention several times during other events leading up to this night. They also claimed their client routinely took selfies with 'fans' and was known for his generosity in helping other wannabe influencers gain a foothold in the ever-increasing competition for followers.

Vines' own testimony detailed how he and Linda, a makeup artist by trade, had a long conversation that night about her ideas and aspiration to launch her own brand range of cosmetics onto the Irish market.

He'd denied being sexually attracted to her, insisting instead that he was 'taken by her energy.' And claimed that the idea of going back to his place was all Linda's, hoping to discuss further.

'I was enjoying the night, we all were. There was an open bar for VIPs which she'd managed to blag her way into.'

'You say blag, was this area invitation-only?'

'It's supposed to be, and it started out that way but as the night wore on, the bouncers cared less, and a few thirsty try-hards were allowed up from downstairs.'

'Ms Joyce was one of these ... try-hards?'

'As far as I'm aware. I knew everyone else there - it's a small enough world and lots of us do cross collaborations and stuff.'

'Cross collaborations?'

'You know, share info on what companies are looking for us to endorse products.'

'Could you perhaps give the court an example of this?'

'Sure. Lets say someone with a profile is moving into a place and needs a new bed or whatever ... we often let each other know which furniture companies are open to IM.'

'Could you clarify the meaning of IM for the court?'

'Influencer Marketing.'

'So these companies might then offer a bed at a discount in return for some additional exposure?'

'Not a discount, they would supply it for free, in return for maybe a grid pic or a video post featuring the new bed or whatever, with a positive review.'

'So the quid pro quo is that the company in question benefits from the exposure someone with a high level following such as your own, can bring?'

'Exactly.'

'And presumably the more followers an influencer has, the more value to those 'investing'?'

'Yeah, but it's a little more complicated than that. Profile from podcasts and TV work is huge too.'

'So on the night in question, you and Ms Joyce were at the launch event discussing influencer marketing. What was the gist of your conversation?'

'She was asking about a department store I collaborate with, and mentioned her interest in cosmetics. I told her it's a difficult area to break into and already pretty saturated. Besides that, she just wanted to have fun and take photos to share on her SM.'

'Social Media?'

'Yeah sorry.'

Reilly looked up from the transcript, recalling her reading of Linda's testimony which, while not completely out of step, was very different to Vines' who she'd claimed was arrogant and aloof.

'So the question of the return to your apartment ... can you take me through exactly how it evolved?'

'She was getting very friendly; like I said, I wasn't attracted to her, nor that into it really, as I was just in the mood to party. I mentioned something about a few others coming back to mine, and she asked if she could come along.'

Linda Joyce had in her own testimony, described the event purely as a networking opportunity, and claimed she was already familiar via social media with many in attendance so didn't feel daunted by going along alone.

The remainder of Vines' testimony comprised of his recollection about heading home and Linda being very friendly. In this regard, the defence had lodged some documented WhatsApp messages between Vines and his friends discussing same.

Most of these exchanges were quite benign, except for one in which he had described Linda Joyce as a 'simp'.

The meaning of the phrase was laid out to the court as somebody who tried too hard to attract the opposite sex.

Whereas the prosecution had lodged messages from other friends reading; *'Save some for us,'* and *'Could do with a bitta spit roast,'* etc, in addition to

Vines' replies, claiming *'Pork's up dudes,'* followed by a succession of pig emojis.

For the purposes of the transcript, the terminology had been translated into layman's terms; 'spit roast' being slang for group sex.

Spit roast...

Even more pertinent given Will Vines' state at his apartment yesterday, Reilly mused, where he himself had been quite literally 'roasted'.

It was clear there was plenty of evidence of male bravado and disrespect for women which painted the guy in a bad light; one very different to his clean cut, gentlemanly online persona.

However, the charge made against Vines was sexual assault, as opposed to being a macho ass.

These guys had exchanged drunk messages, never thinking for a second they would be seen by anyone outside of the group, never mind trawled through in a court of law.

Reilly's mind wondered to another high-profile Irish case where the victim had managed to press record on her phone during the assault, and while no images had been captured on camera, the audio alone had been enough to get a rock-solid conviction.

Show, don't tell ...

It was clear that Linda Joyce's biggest problem was that the case was built on her word only. Her delay in reporting the incident until two days later meant there was a lack of physical evidence of any kind.

Apparently she'd been ashamed immediately after the incident, and it was only after confiding in a friend that she'd worked up the courage to come forward about the assault.

Plus the potential threat of a resultant social media storm and backlash had also weighed heavy on her mind at the time.

Reilly herself recalled a few related news reports and social media commentary which had ultimately driven Linda Joyce to the darkest of places.

Witnesses were also unhelpful to her case; Vines' friends arrived at his apartment only after she had left.

The taxi driver who took her home could corroborate her story about being upset, but this couldn't be attributed to a violent assault, and was indeed passed off by the defence as a case of distraught stemming from his disinterest in her.

'Mr Vines, the prosecution claims that shortly after you returned to your apartment and ascertained that it was empty save for the two of you, you proceeded to coerce Ms Joyce to, firstly perform a sexual act before insisting on penetrative sex - despite her clear protestations.'

'That's complete lies, it never happened. I wouldn't have had sex with Linda Joyce if she was the last girl alive'.

Reilly looked up.

Vines' last line struck home - she'd read that somewhere before.

She picked up another file from her desk that Rory had since compiled and opened it.

Inside, were several opinion pieces by the journalist David Walsh, along with printouts of tweets and other potentially inflammatory social media correspondence.

She flicked through some of the sheets until she found the one she wanted.

'Case Closed. We need new legislation in Ireland to prevent decent men having their reputations slaughtered by hearsay. #lastgirlalive

A popular Irish male faces an uncertain future, having seen brands disassociate themselves because of a weak, fickle accusation that has cast an eerie shadow over his reputation. Do you think it's time to ensure a minimum evidential requirement for legal proceedings, and a right to claim damages for false claims? Poll below.

The replies and comments beneath were a toxic mix of gender division and downright hate; a couple of hashtags in particular becoming synonymous with opposing sides; #IBelieveHer in support of Linda Joyce, and #LastGirlAlive for those siding with Vines and the general outcry against groundless male accusations by the opposite sex.

Reilly reread one of Walsh's articles relating to the court case. While no names were mentioned, it was blatantly obvious to all who the main players were. And unusual to read a piece with zero empathy for the alleged victim.

She had of course since learned that Will Vines

and David Walsh were friendly socially and with this in mind, it was now all too easy to read between the lines.

Walsh's main argument was that the man's career was in jeopardy over claims that should never have come before a judge and jury, painting Vines as the victim and casting Linda Joyce as the villain.

In doing so, David Walsh had unwittingly made himself a target of online abuse, but his devastating hashtag had it seemed, been the final straw for Joyce.

Vine's not-guilty verdict and the associated shame of having her reputation dragged through the mud - plus her name going viral as the ubiquitous 'last girl alive' - appeared to have ultimately driven poor Linda Joyce to take her own life.

30

That afternoon, the detectives drove to the Westside Plaza Hotel.

'Drive round the side,' Chris instructed, spotting the sign for the entrance to the adjoining Renaissance Body and Soul Spa.

'Not too shabby...'

'No expense spared for the former Mrs Shaughnessy apparently.'

Kennedy drove into a vacant parking space amongst an expensive array of high-end SUVs and sports cars. 'What's the deal here do we know? Joint venture between herself and Seanie?' he asked.

Chris folded himself gingerly out of the Ford that looked like a right banger alongside the other luxury badges on display. Still, he figured at least it was a lot safer here than outside Lynch's place in the Valley.

'He was named as an original director on

company records, but it was always Carolyn's baby. Her ex just helped finance it.'

The two headed toward the spa; the entryway framed by a striped purple and white awning, with expensive marble paving beneath leading to a brass revolving door which wouldn't look out of place in Manhattan.

Kennedy stood aside to let him through the door first, silently acknowledging that he would be taking the lead on this one.

Jim Lynch was no fool. The fact he had brought up Sean Shaughnessy's ex-wife's name was noteworthy. From what little information Chris had gleaned, the split had been quite toxic.

And places like this didn't come cheap, even for well-connected solicitors.

Part of him wondered if the divorce had caused some kind of upheaval to Lynch's operations - and initiating such a visit was somehow related. The organised crime boss had suddenly become a lot more vulnerable since his solicitor's passing, and thus his means of legitimising various business interests, considerably harder.

Was this an attempt by Lynch to pressurise Sean's ex into facilitating some laundering thing he had going on?

'Here to see Carolyn Smith,' Kennedy informed a young girl behind the front desk - a glowing rectangular cuboid that resembled a Himalayan salt wall.

No expense spared.

'Ms Smith is just finishing up on a call; I'll announce your arrival once she is ready.'

The detectives were duly led up a sleek glass staircase into yet another plush mezzanine area. The waiting room, also expensively furnished, was positioned across from a wall-to-ceiling slate water feature dominating the double height space down to the entrance floor.

The scent of essential oils permeated throughout, making Chris's eyes water.

'All a bit Hollywood try-hard, isn't it?' Kennedy muttered, wrinkling his nose.

'People pay a fortune for this stuff, sure none of us ever need to worry about looking all wrinkly anymore,' Chris joked, referring to a nearby audiovisual screen detailing the various beauty treatments on offer.

'Good morning Detectives, would you like to come on through?' came a smooth voice from a nearby doorway.

Carolyn Smith was a trim, tanned, and deeply attractive blonde in her early forties, dressed in a black jumpsuit and metallic heels. Beckoning them inside another plushly furnished space, she gestured for them to take a seat on a pair of stylish purple suede egg chairs.

As the former Mrs Shaughnessy took her own seat across from them, Chris noticed sparkling jewellery on her arms as she perched them on the white onyx desk, backlit like the one in reception.

'Can I offer you some refreshments? Herbal tea or oxygenated water?'

'You're grand thanks love,' Kennedy answered for both of them, as Chris smiled inwardly.

'So how can I help you today?' Carolyn sat back in her seat, a diamond ring the size of a small helicopter also glittering beneath the overhead lighting.

'We just wanted to ask a couple of questions about your recently deceased ex-husband.'

Chris observed her reaction.

Carolyn knew exactly why they were here, but her body language when faced with questioning would be just as informative as the words coming out of her mouth.

She unfolded her arms and stretched them out on the table surface, as if bracing herself off of it. 'How can I help?'

'When was the last time you spoke to Sean?'

She tilted her head to the ceiling and focused her eyes into the middle distance, deep in thought.

'Probably about four months ago when I needed some documents signed for the business.'

'This business?'

'Yes.'

'Was that in person?'

'Over the phone - I had the documents sent to Maura. Sean and I haven't met in person since our divorce hearing last year.'

'Was the spit amicable?' Kennedy asked directly.

She squirmed a little and pursed her lips. 'Maybe for him it was. Sorry detectives, I'm just not sure how this ancient history has anything to do with my ex-husband's recent passing.'

'We just need to establish a few things is all, just standard practice,' Kennedy soothed.

'So, it wasn't ... amicable for you?' Chris probed, already knowing some background about this former power couple who'd lived life in the open world of the Dublin social scene.

'Divorcing a solicitor is never easy, Detective'.

'I can imagine. So when was the last time you saw him, other than at the hearing?'

She exhaled. 'A Christmas fundraiser at the Shelbourne shortly before that - we didn't speak. He was with one of his ... girlfriends.'

Chris knew of the solicitor's playboy reputation, as did everybody else. 'That part of the reason for the split?'

Carolyn sat upright in the chair, re-folding her arms defensively. 'Detective I'm actually not at all comfortable with this line of questioning. I agreed to see you today out of courtesy and without my solicitor present.'

Her complexion reddened in annoyance.

'Yes, and we appreciate that - again we're just trying to get a sense of Sean's broader social circle so as to better ascertain who might have had reason to hurt him. I'm sure you understand. For what it's worth, you're not under any suspicion here.'

'I should hope not.' Carolyn shook her head dismissively. 'It's already common knowledge that Sean was a ladies' man. We grew apart and when I was ready to move on, I did. He wasn't happy and tried to take my business - the one thing he knew I cared most about, out of spite or bruised ego, who knows? All I know is I went through hell to keep this place.'

'Again, we're just trying to piece together a complicated picture to help find out who killed your ex husband and given Sean's varied business ... connections - it's not an easy task.'

'I don't envy your job, I really don't. There were two distinct sides to Sean; the man I met back in school who wanted to change the world, and the man I divorced who was indeed doing that. He created his fair share of enemies over the years as I'm sure you can also imagine.'

'Would you be willing to help us identify some of these enemies? Particularly any who might've been willing to have him killed.'

'Come on Detectives, you know all too well who Sean rolled with. You choose to lie with snakes, eventually you'll get bitten. And I myself lived with one for far too long.'

'What about Jim Lynch? Would he be one of those snakes you're referring to?' Chris ventured.

Immediately her demeanour changed at the mention of the crime boss.

There was something there all right...

She sighed deeply. 'I might have known he'd try this.'

'Who?' he asked, all-innocence.

'Jim. We had an ... understanding at one point, he and I. It's the only reason Sean backed down from trying to take everything from me.'

'What kind of understanding?'

'Well, if you must know ...' Carolyn looked ashamed. 'I'm not proud of it, but I knew Jim was ... interested in me. So I used that to get him to persuade Sean to ... simplify our divorce.'

'And has this understanding with Lynch continued?' Kennedy asked then.

'Absolutely not - it was leverage pure and simple. But that wasn't enough for Jim. Which I suspect is why he sent you two here to try to punish me for that. And like fools, you took the bait.'

'I'm afraid you're going to have to explain further...'

'Detective, I was married to a solicitor remember?' Carolyn shot back, eyes gleaming, and Chris understood that she truly wasn't a woman to be trifled with. Especially not if she'd got the better of a man like Jim Lynch, or indeed her ex husband.

'I know my rights. I had no quarrel with Sean, other than the fact that he once tried to take this place from me. And he kept me in the dark about any other of his business interests so to speak, because that was exactly how I wanted it. We've long cut ties since the divorce. And I've long cut ties with his friends too,' she added, evidently referring to Lynch. 'That's all I've got to say on the matter. If you want further assistance from me, it'll need to be through legal channels.'

She got to her feet, indicating the end of their chat, as the two detectives stood up in tandem.

'One more thing,' Chris asked as he turned towards the door. 'At Sean's funeral, you seemed ... upset for someone who'd long cut ties.'

'You honestly expected me to be cheering?' Carolyn said, tears in her eyes, and despite her hostile demeanour, he believed her sincerity. 'Sean was many things, but when all is said and done he was once my husband, and my first love. That was the man I mourned - unlike his dolly-birds bawling over the loss of their sugar daddy.'

31

Lucy moved the specimen around under the microscope in order to view it from another angle. She was certain her hunch was correct.

The evidence retrieved from the ensuite in William Vines' apartment was crystalline and colourless. Its surface features were hard to determine since the sample was minuscule, but she had tested enough of this in the past to be fairly confident that what she was looking at was glass.

The sample size would restrict her from any thickness analysis, so she examined it closely from a number of angles. The fluorescence indicated it was from a flat surface as opposed to something curved such as a car windscreen or a drinking glass.

'What have you got?' Gary asked, walking up beside her and making her jump slightly.

'Flipping hell, you frightened the shit out of me.'

'Sorry, it's just ... I recognise that look.' She stood back, indicating the sample and he duly put an eye to it. 'What is it?'

'Glass. From Vines' place. 'No curvature and under the UV lamp there was fluorescence.'

'You'll have to fill me in on what that means ...'

'Well, you know the way Reilly always says the floor beneath broken glass is never truly clean and it's impossible to fully clear up immediately after; there's always remnants left behind?' Lucy leaned back against a desk to take the weight off her tired limbs before continuing. 'From the outset, I was pretty sure it was glass, but it was the only piece found in Vines' place.'

'So you don't think it came from any actual glass breakage in his apartment?'

'Correct. There was a couple of dirty glasses catalogued but pristine so it obviously didn't come from those. And according to the flatmate, there was a cleaner in the day before he left. So could this have been walked in from outside?' she pondered. 'Lack of curvature would indicate it wasn't from a rounded drinking glass. And the fluorescence also indicates the presence of tin.'

'Tin?'

'Yes. When the kind of glass used for windows and doors is manufactured, they use a float process, where liquid glass is poured onto molten tin. The surface immediately in contact with the tin during manufacture will fluoresce when exposed to short-wave UV light.'

'Right, so you mean glass from a broken door or window?'

'Perhaps, but impossible to get a more detailed profile without using destructive testing.'

'So it doesn't really give us anything then ... what?' he urged, confused at her wry smile, like she was waiting for the penny to drop.

'It doesn't give us anything *unless* we have comparative samples.'

'Shaughnessy's door...' he said, finally catching onto her thought process.

'Exactly, we never analysed that because we already knew the source. So if we're operating on the assumption that our doer was at both scenes, we can compare the samples without worrying about destroying them. *Which* is what I was about to do before you came over, but now that you're here you can give me a hand.'

She instructed Gary to fetch the equipment and they cleared a space at a different work station with a gas burner.

'OK, so talk me through it.'

'Comparative Refractive Index Test or CRIT. If I put a piece of glass into water, you can still see the glass because the water and glass have different refractive indices, yes?' Lucy said, as she filled a beaker and carefully placed a glass sample taken from Sean Shaughnessy's back door into it.

'And now if we put this piece of glass from Will Vines' apartment in, we can still see that also. Heating the water to a certain temperature, the refractive indices of the water and the glass should be the same - and if the glass is of the same composition, we should no longer be able to see both pieces either.'

'So if one piece becomes invisible, and the other remains, they are from a different source, if they become invisible at the same time ...'

'They're both likely from the same source or similar,' Lucy finished his sentence, just as the two pieces in the slowly heating water gradually became indistinguishable to the naked eye at exactly the same time as the other.

Gary brought his face closer to ascertain for sure that he couldn't see either, before looking up at her. 'You sure this isn't cross contamination?'

'Can't be one hundred percent positive obviously. Unlikely to have come from us though, given protocol. Same for M.E. Plus the fact it was found in Vines' en suite and I'm pretty certain we were the first in there. Greg didn't even reach it in time to spew in the toilet.'

Lucy looked at him. 'If I were a betting woman, I'd be putting my house on that transference coming from someone - besides the authorities - who was present at both sites.'

32

'Mama, there's a strange dog running around outside with Buster and Otto.'

Lina duly got to her feet and went towards the window where Emmy was standing. Cici ran to join them and the three stared perplexed as their two German Shepherds charged around with a stray.

The other dogs seemed as surprised as the three onlookers at the pale golden retriever bouncing around, trying to instigate play.

It barked then bolted off, stopping and turning to encourage the others to join in. They had never been encouraged to play having been engaged for one purpose only; protection.

When they were pups Lina had worked hard to not let the girls turn them into pets. They were working dogs who would earn their keep by adding to Layer One.

Now as the girls laughed at the antics of this playful visitor a knot of worry began to form. How had that mutt gotten in? She and Peter had designed the house and surrounding area to be impenetrable.

Two layers of dense, thorny vegetation with a drainage ditch that was actually not designed to drain but collect water. A steel security fence with anti-climbing technology that would cause any would-be intruders to lose their fingers should they deign to climb over.

The fence was obscured on either side with thick bramble bushes to soften the industrial look. It also acted as a source of blackberries they used along with the other fruit they grew to make jams and tarts.

The main route in and out by vehicle was via one set of gates at the bottom of the lane, and another by way of the security fence closer to the house and farm buildings.

She moved towards the kitchen worktop where about the only piece of modern-day technology was kept, striking a few keys until a screen split evenly in four displaying live footage appeared. She exhaled deeply upon seeing two of the CCTV camera images showing both sets of gates firmly closed.

The other two images were panoramic shots of the front and back of the house and her attention was caught by brief movement as the three dogs continued to run around, becoming acquainted with each other.

'Oh he's so cute - just a pup really. Can we keep him?' Cici asked, over her shoulder.

Lina didn't answer as she wracked her brains trying to figure out how the intruder had gained entry.

She pulled on her boots and jacket and picked up the loaded rifle that hung beside the back door.

'Where are you going?'

'Stay inside, both of you and lock the door,' she warned, then seeing the panic in her daughters' faces she felt immediately guilty. 'It's OK. I'm just going to check the area, see if I can find out how the dog got in. He looks far too well-groomed to be a stray.'

Lina scolded herself for being so reactionary. They had always planned that if anyone did try to gain access they would discourage a stand off.

The first rule of survival in an intrusion should always be a smile and a welcome.

With just her and a couple of teenagers alone in the house, aggression would not be an option.

Disarm with a smile, befriend with kindness, expel by stealth.

Peter always maintained it would be easier to get rid of somebody after gaining their trust rather than head-on aggression.

Lina hadn't yet had the opportunity to try out the potions she'd derived from various plants and fungi, but knew she wouldn't hesitate to use them to incapacitate if needed.

Though not in this case.

Outside, she made her way between the farm buildings that led to the paddocks where the sheep and some new lambs were grazing in the evening sunshine, and could hear the pigs rummaging and snorting in their shed nearby.

It took her a few minutes to walk to the boundary beyond the paddocks, and would take her many more to walk the full perimeter.

She decided to walk to the gate first; it being the obvious weak link.

Lina continued to walk, stooping down on occasion to look through any potential holes in the brambles where a dog may have squeezed through. Before they had dogs, foxes would often burrow under the fence and steal chickens.

A little while later, she was none the wiser as to how the stray had gained entry. She figured it must have squeezed under the fence somehow.

As she walked back up to the house the girls appeared, and all three dogs came over in a blur of wagging tails and lolling tongues.

'He's on his own, can we keep him?' Cici pleaded again.

'It has a collar and a tag,' Lina said putting her had down and stroking the animal while turning over his name tag to reveal the name 'Bailey.' 'Somebody will come looking for it.'

She decided not to read out or mention a name, knowing that would only make things harder when it was time to dispose of the animal.

Then above the dogs growling and play-acting, she thought she heard a noise.

'Shhh, listen,' she said as the girls fell silent. In the distance they could hear a voice.

'I hear someone calling,' Cici said, crouching down between Otto and the stray. 'Calling Bailey.'

Reading the name tag for herself she quickly put two and two together.

'Inside,' Lina ordered as she herded the girls back into the house, beckoning Bailey in behind her for before it began responding to the calls of its master.

Once inside, she looked at the CCTV screen, horrified afresh to see a car parked up, and its occupant examining the exterior as if looking for a bell or intercom.

'Girls ...' Lina warned firmly. 'Stay here and keep that dog inside.'

Again she headed down the driveway, punching in the code to open the first set of gates, before proceeding through to the laneway as they closed behind her.

Inside, the girls looked on, first out the window as the gates closed and then on the footage of the lower gate and the stranger trying to find a way in.

They continued to watch with rising levels of anxiety as they saw their mother appear on screen and start to converse with the man.

After some back and forth, with their mother seeming to point up the road as if giving directions, they breathed a sigh of relief.

Then Lina could be seen waving and walking away as the man got into his car and drove off.

The girls moved to the window just in time to see their mother walking through and the gate closing shut behind her.

'What did that man want?' Cici asked.

'Don't be stupid, what do you think he wanted, he was looking for the dog,' Emmy retorted. 'Does this mean we can keep him?' her sister asked hopefully, stroking Bailey's thick coat.

Lina shook her head. 'No, he'd just be another mouth to feed. Plus Buster and Otto might forget their purpose.'

'Why didn't you bring Bailey to the man then?'

'I wanted to get rid of him first and foremost. Far easier to deny knowledge than engage in discussion and invite too many questions. Plus I'd have had to open the gate. I wasn't willing to do that, who knows who he was or what he was after.

'What about Bailey then?'

'Who's being stupid now? The dog can't stay and the dog can't go ... use your brain,' Emmy scoffed. 'I'll do it Mama, I know what has to be done,' she added and Lina nodded.

'What? No ...' Cici protested.

C'mon it's only a stupid mutt. How are you going to cope in this world when the change comes?' Emmy scorned.

'Leave her be,' Lina instructed, as she attached a

rope to Bailey's collar and the dog duly followed her youngest to the back door.

Whereupon Emmy already had the rifle out and held the door open as the retriever wandered through it, wagging expectantly.

33

Kennedy pulled up outside his house and parked the car outside the gate because the driveway was already full.

Not recognising the extra two cars, he inwardly hoped that Josie wasn't hosting her book club. The thought of an evening of wine-fuelled cackling was nearly enough to make him get back in the car and drive back to work.

He turned his key in the front door and pushed it open to be greeted by voices coming from the kitchen, and immediately deciphered the chatter of his eldest teenage daughter and her friends.

'Hey, where's your Mum?'

'In the sitting room I think,' Selena replied, with less than usual cheeriness. He noticed that all the girls looked a bit glum as they sat around the kitchen island stroking their phones.

'Everything all right?'

'We're just upset about Willy.'

'Sorry wha...?' he asked, totally thrown by this.

'Will ...Vines?'

'Oh right yeah. Nasty business.'

'You're working on that case, Dad, aren't you? Any idea who did it?'

He exhaled loudly. 'Pet, you know I don't discuss work at home. Or can't. But rest assured everything's in hand and it's early days yet.'

He made a hasty retreat and headed for the living room where he could see the flickering of the TV inside.

'Oh hello love, I wasn't sure if it was yourself. How was your day?' Josie asked.

'Long,' Kennedy slumped into the couch beside his beloved wife and gave her a peck on the cheek.

'You hungry?'

'After all these years, you still ask me that question even though I've only ever given you one answer.'

'There's lasagne in the oven. I'll try to clear the mourners from the kitchen first,' she chuckled, pushing herself out of the seat, and his mouth watered like Pavlov's dog, even though he'd already had a grand feed after interviewing Shaughnessy's ex earlier. But he wouldn't be admitting that, and anyway it already felt like donkeys' years ago.

'The girls are having a bit of a JFK/Lady Di

moment. I'd never heard of the fella myself, had you?'

'Are you joking me? But I've now a new list of words to add to my vocabulary, did you know what an influencer or a vlogger is?'

'Not really, do I need to?'

'Nope.'

'Good, I'll give you a shout when it's on the table.'

'Cheers love,' Kennedy sat back on the sofa, picked up the remote and changed stations from the lifestyle show Josie had been watching, to the main evening news.

Chris's TV2 reporter friend was standing outside William Vines' apartment block, the same huge candle-lit vigil taking place for the second night running.

The screen then flashed to archive footage taken several months before of a freshly-vindicated Vines and his solicitor Sean Shaughnessy on the steps of the High Court making a statement.

While as expected, the report strongly intimated the link between the two recently-deceased men as potential fallout from the rape trial.

O'Brien would go ape ...

Vines had been found not guilty, but by all accounts the verdict had led to the plaintiff Linda Joyce going on to take her own life.

And while the trial itself had been behind closed doors, on social media, it seemed nothing was sacred. Having sat through a few assault proceedings in his time, Kennedy didn't even want to imagine what it had been like for the girl, first to have her character decimated throughout, and then have to contend with all these unfounded rumours and accusations flying around willy-nilly online.

And the poor girl wasn't much older than his Selena.

Then he sat up straight in his seat, as something else in the news footage caught his eye. Lifting up the remote, he rewinded and replayed the section again, before pausing, where in the background Linda Joyce, shielded and surrounded by family, could be seen exiting the court building.

He took his phone from his pocket and unlocked it before scrolling through some images. Then he quickly dialled Chris's number and waited impatiently for him to pick up.

'Did you see the news just now?'

'No, what's happened?' Chris asked.

'Sarah's following up on the trial thing, yeah?'

'Said she spoke to the father earlier - he's coming in for a chat tomorrow.'

'What about the brothers?'

'Not sure, I think she said one's working abroad and the other's in uni. Why?'

'Fairly certain one of them is our runner from yesterday - just spotted him in the background of old footage from that trial. Have a look and ring me back.'

Kennedy hung up just as Josie called him, and he pressed record on the news to have another look later before cheerfully following the smell of food wafting in from the kitchen - like a rat lining up behind the Pied Piper.

34

While Selena's friends had gone home, she was still hanging around while he ate his grub, and Kennedy wasn't sure if he was imagining it but she seemed to be paying a lot more attention to him than normal, albeit with her head still buried in her phone.

'How was your day pet?' he asked her, as Josie placed his dinner in front of him.

'OK, considering ...' Selena replied without raising her eyes.

'Did you tell Dad about the test?' Josie prompted.

'Oh yeah, I got a date for my driving test - the third of next month.'

'No bother to you pet, you take after me.'

'Did you even do a test? Grandad said years ago they gave out driving licences to whoever wanted one.'

'They actually did, well before my time, mind.

Try to get out a bit more from now until your test, OK?'

Selena nodded and then cursed under her breath at her phone.

'I really wish you would put that blasted thing away at the table, it's so antisocial,' Josie scolded as she sipped her cup of tea.

'I won't sit at the table then,' her daughter said petulantly. She stood up and walked over to the fridge where she took out a can of Coke and started to drink it while still engrossed in the phone.

'What's so important anyway?' Kennedy asked, to defuse any potential aggro.

'That bitch, Suzi Cox is doubling-down on what she's been saying about Will.'

'Language, Selena ...' Josie scolded.

'Bitch isn't a swear word though.'

'Unless this Suzi Cox is actually a female dog it is, but dogs don't have social media.'

'They do actually, you know that terrier that ran onto the pitch during the Dubs game at the weekend? Has its own TikTok now,' she said smugly.

'World's gone stone mad.' Kennedy groaned. 'Tell us, what's the deal with this Will fella anyway? Tragic what happened to him, but I'm struggling to understand the level of upset since he was up to some shady shenanigans it seems.'

Selena walked back over to the table, and the fact that she hadn't already disappeared up to her room told him she wanted to talk about it.

No harm, it might give him a better bit of insight into the kind of world they were dealing with for this investigation. As it was, he felt a bit clueless about all this and was much more at home with the likes of Jim Lynch or even Shaughnessy's ex, more straightforward stuff. This social media craic was more of a young man's - or indeed woman's - game.

'Just because he wasn't perfect doesn't mean people shouldn't be upset,' Selena replied, fresh tears in her eyes. 'Will gave so much of himself online, we all felt like we knew him, that he was a friend even.'

'Fair enough love, it's just a bit harder for an old codger like me to understand,' he replied. 'But that whole nasty business he was involved in too, surely that put a few people off?'

'He was cleared of that in court, you above all people should understand that. Anyway everybody knows he wasn't into girls like ... her. That hashtag was right.'

'I don't follow ...'

Selena stared at him. 'The hashtag that was going around during the trial? I know it was supposed to be secret but some journalist leaked the expression, and it went viral. Will said he wouldn't have gone near that girl even if she was the last girl alive.'

Some journalist ...

Now his mind raced even further. 'What journalist - can you remember?'

'Dunno. Just some guy that Suzi Cox hates too -

she was always roasting him on Twitter. I can't remember. Anyway, she's just a troll, looking for attention.'

'Could it be David Walsh?'

'Yep, that's the one. Those two were always at it during the trial. The Feminazi versus The Masculinist.'

'The what?'

'Feminazi, militant feminist-slash-manhater.'

Kennedy could figure that bit out, but what or who the hell a masculinist was, he had no idea.

'Other men calling out the feminists, picking holes in their stupid arguments,' Selena explained. 'It got nasty during Will's court case. The journalist guy leaked the hashtag and because everyone knew it was about the girl, Suzi Cox went apeshit.'

Interesting... He was sure Sarah would likely be all over this, and it certainly tied together a few more strands in this investigation.

'So do you know who killed Will yet?' his daughter asked.

'Come on pet, you know I can't discuss those details with you.'

Selena nodded and lifted up the phone again, unable to resist, as a tone alerted her to yet another new notification. She chuckled as she read. 'Ha, serves her right.'

'Serves who right?' Josie asked.

'Suzi Cox, look - a picture of her car covered in red paint outside the TV studio.'

Josie harrumphed. 'That's not nice Selena, how would you like it. And speaking of hashtags, whatever happened to 'be kind'?'

'*I'm* not the one spreading hate, Mum.'

'Your mam's right - people are entitled to their opinion. Some smartarse threw paint at this one's house already too apparently,' Kennedy revealed, and Josie shook her head as Selena failed to conceal a smirk. 'Tell you one thing, if you ever get involved with any of that kind of shenanigans we'll be changing the locks and you'll be on your own.'

'Seriously?' Selena huffed, pushing back from the table.

'I'm just saying, since your own father is a detective on this case I'd hope that you wouldn't involve yourself with any of those behaviours you seem to be condoning.'

'Oh, I see. It would reflect badly on your precious job ... I get it,' his daughter replied insolently as she headed for the kitchen door.

'Don't be a smartarse, you know what I mean,' Kennedy reiterated, his face reddening as she stomped out of the room. He was about to get to his feet to follow her, when Josie reached across and placed a calming hand on his.

As she did so often these days.

35

'Well?'

'Looks like him all right. Seems like it's the younger brother, the one in college,' Chris said calling his partner back while Kennedy sat in his study, where he'd retreated after dinner.

'Are we going to put a warrant out? Reasonable suspicion should do it - he did run.'

'Yeah but I was never really that close - any solicitor worth his salt would claim he was just in a rush somewhere and didn't hear me calling him. I'll check if anything from the bike lock, though the letter that was sent to Douglas should be enough to put the frighteners on him.'

'Let's bring him in so. And while I have you, Selena told me some interesting tidbits about your woman Cox. Misfortunate surname considering ...'

Chris chuckled. 'Better not let her hear you say that.

Hanging up, Kennedy immediately entered the names of the aforementioned journalists into a search engine, and was quickly confronted with multiple links to various social media sites, think-pieces and news articles listing both names.

It was apparent that the two had crossed swords on numerous occasions. One article written by Walsh grabbed his attention: *When the equality movement tips the scales.*

Kennedy read the piece which was basically a labelling of modern feminism 'as a false flag for an anti male agenda.'

Whatever the hell that meant.

Walsh banged on about the emasculation of modern men who lived in a world where to show mere interest in a member of the opposite sex could land him in jail.

Kennedy scrolled down to the comments section and was amazed to find several hundred responses. Reading a few, it didn't take long to get the sense that there was a lot of anger and hate, people saying things to each other online that would never have been uttered directly.

He sat back in his chair, wondering when had life become so complicated.

It was as if evolution had sped up in the last decade to the point where everybody had two separate personas now - one online and the other in the real world. The trouble was some people didn't seem to know where one ended and the other began.

He opened the file he'd brought home to review and started to flick through it, stopping at the footage assembled in relation to the runner down at the docks yesterday.

Then he googled the assault victim Linda Joyce, and came across her Facebook account, which had since become more of a memorial page.

Mostly messages of condolence addressing her personally, and he felt a little spooked reading them. Seeing pictures of the deceased smiling with friends in happier times, the whole thing made for tragic viewing.

He clicked on a 'friend' link and scrolled through until he found an account for one of the brothers - Ben, Chris had said his name was.

Posts about college events and sports teams along with funny clips involving cerebrally challenged teenagers up to stupid shenanigans and coming off the worst for it.

The way it should be.

Kennedy looked at an image of a group of five lads, arms around each other wearing big smiles on a night out in some bar.

The brother was in the middle. Was this young fella a killer, driven to avenge his sister?

What would it take to drive what looked like a normal young man to such extreme measures?

Kennedy was unsure but he was glad that they

had made some progress, and now at least had a suspect with cause enough to detain.

He sent a decent picture of the guy from the Facebook page to the family printer, along with the shot he'd already printed of yesterday's CCTV footage of the runner to take to the office tomorrow.

There was little doubt they were one and the same person.

Now all they had to do was place the brother at any of the recent crime scenes, and they were away.

36

Reilly picked up the evidence bags containing the bedding from Will Vines' apartment, plus the clothing he'd been wearing while essentially being roasted alive.

She carried them over to an empty examination table and grabbing her evidence retrieval kit, removed a pair of latex gloves and put them on.

Carefully opening the first bag, she tipped the contents - a heavy duvet - onto the table.

The first thing to hit her was the strong smell of human excrement. The last dying act of any human had a particularly pungent odour, made all the worse by containment in an oxygen-starved plastic bag.

She immediately noted there was no strong smell of ammonia one would normally associate with the emptying of the bladder, also usual at death, but in this instance was unsurprised given the influencer's ultimate cause of death was dehydration and organ failure.

She spread the duvet out, careful not to dislodge any potential trace, and was also glad this particular piece of bedding had been on top of the corpse, as opposed to beneath, so she didn't have to contend with those final expulsions as yet.

Reilly reached across and pulled a large magnifying glass with a powerful ring light much like the ones found in fancy hotel bathrooms for close up eyebrow plucking. Or indeed by image-conscious influencers filming themselves for content.

The magi-lite attached to the edge of the examination table had a multi directional arm which allowed her to place it in the required position, while leaving her hands free to examine the duvet.

She quickly spied some bodily strands and fibres which she removed with a tweezer and placed individually into glass slides for closer examination. Then having searched every square inch of the duvet for more obvious trace, Reilly went about locating the less obvious and far more valuable kind.

Placing the tweezers back into their slot in her kitbag, she removed a roll of tape and set about examining the bedcover again, this time looking for anything too small for manual extraction.

She came across a couple of areas of interest and proceeded to remove a piece of clear tape from a roll sticky on one side and in predetermined lengths of three centimetres to match the length of a microscope slide.

She very gently positioned the tape onto an area in which she could see a faint deposit of loose material, and ran her gloved finger along the non-sticky surface, before retrieving her tweezers once more to carefully remove it before placing it in a slide.

Reilly repeated this procedure several times until the holder was full with thirty individual slides. She closed the lid and taking a sharpie marker from her bag, labelled the box.

She continued the procedure on the underside of the duvet and by the time she was finished she'd collected several boxes.

When she was done collecting trace evidence by sight, Reilly picked up the Wet Vac and pressed the on button. The extraction tool sparked into life and she used the nozzle to lightly vacuum the entire duvet.

The Wet Vac system was a recent addition to the lab with the aim of locating previously undetectable potential DNA sources from upholstery or clothing.

The nozzle was attached to a hose feeding into a machine that looked like a mini kidney dialysis unit. Sterile water was fed from a container similar to an IV bag and pumped via the nozzle whereupon it was expelled into the material being treated.

The water was then sucked back into the hose where it was passed through a filter which collected any finer trace for further analysis. Like a more modern day version of panning for gold - which in forensic terms, was about the same.

She carried out a similar procedure on the rest of the bedding and then clothing from the victim himself. By the time she had finished she had multiple swabs, boxes of slides and several Wet Vac filters all labeled and ready for further analysis.

The crew were going to just love the extra workload plus additional lab hours sifting through all this entailed. But that was the job.

Happy with her efforts, she repacked everything up and carried the tray of slide boxes over to her desk where she would make a head-start herself in the hope of narrowing down anything of interest.

Enough to justify further examination on microspec or other specialist equipment that might help identify this stuff and contribute anything worthy to the investigation.

She placed the filters from the Wet-Vac aside to process later with a DNA extraction kit, and started to look through the slides, taking notes and numbering them as she went.

Reilly glanced around the lab. Everyone else was head-down, deep in their own work.

She saw Gary's head bobbing up and down with his earbuds in, listening to the nineties music he so enjoyed.

When he'd first started doing this, she hadn't been so sure, but his work and results had shown that the music was of no distraction, and no small relief to the others, now spared of his dubious taste.

She looked at her watch, eleven thirty. Just enough time before the detectives were due to arrive around noon.

As she went through the slides taking notes on each, one in particular caught her eye. That loose dusty material that she had collected from the duvet.

Placing it under the lens, she upped the magnification and adjusted the lighting.

The dust on the slide was organic in nature but not immediately identifiable. The M.E's office had yet to furnish a tox report for Vines, but Reilly already suspected there must have been something used to subdue the victim.

Two used glasses had been in William Vines' apartment, but had both been wiped clean.

Now, looking at under the microscope, the material appeared to be some sort of powder. A potential drug or sedative perhaps?

Either way it was interesting enough for further investigation.

She set about preparing a sample plug for insertion into the spectrometer which would give her the answer she needed.

The complicated setting of the sample for injection took some time. She worked steadily and methodically through the process before commencing. The results would be sent to print and require comparative analysis at a later stage.

For now though, the growling in her stomach could no longer be ignored. She reset the machine and organised her work station so that everything was stored properly.

Then headed to her office and retrieved her phone to see that she had several missed calls.

And a message from none other than Daniel Forrest.

In the 'hood on Friday for a lecture. Dinner?

She figured that this apparent out of the blue contact from her mentor (and grandfather of her child if things had worked out) or indeed appearance in the city, wasn't quite as casual as he was making it sound.

Daniel had of course been in touch after the ... incident, but she hadn't exactly been in a frame of mind to discuss it, having already had to negotiate a difficult and emotional conversation with Todd.

A rush of fresh gratitude flooded through her now at how Chris had been there to help her through the worst of it, and she knew deep down that she had indeed been unfair to him in pushing him away.

She needed to make amends, but for the moment figured she should get the Daniel thing over and done with.

While he'd always been a natural father figure, and she enjoyed his company, she knew his visit was sure to unearth the kind of emotions she was trying her utmost to keep buried.

Not sure - busy caseload just now, she replied.

His response came back immediately:

Nice try. I'd really love to see you - even for a half hour if you can spare. Call you when I'm in town? P.S. No pressure.

She sent a single emoji 'fingers crossed' reply, deciding to just park the decision for a bit and tackle later whether or not she wanted to see him - or indeed if she had the time.

Then scrolling through her other notifications, she saw three recent missed calls from Chris.

'Hey, you were looking for me? I thought you guys were coming in at twelve.'

'We're just across in Brogan's grabbing a bite beforehand, just wanted to see if you wanted to join us?'

She was relieved his tone sounded breezy and normal, so at least he seemed to be over ... whatever had gone down last week.

'Sounds good, order me the lasagne, I'll be there in five.'

37

Brogan's was what Kennedy described as a proper 'oul fellas pub' not far from the GFU building.

Walking in, Reilly looked around to see him and Chris already tucking into plates of mouthwatering home style cooking she would gladly have wrestled them for.

The pub was busy with the last of the lunchtime trade finishing up.

Being this close to the lab, there was usually lots of familiar faces. The staff buzzed around, and the smell of coffee filled the air.

Pubs in Ireland at this time of day were definitely more restaurants than drinking establishments, but Reilly often thought if this place could talk it would have some interesting stories to tell. The old oak bar was almost an antique, as were the elaborate optics holder and built in shelves and mirrors behind it.

'Busy morning?' Chris asked by way of greeting.

She nodded. 'You could say that ...'

'Any scoop for us yet - preferably something to make it handy and lead us right to our man like they do on the telly,' Kennedy drawled.

'I wish. We're still ploughing through all. How about you?'

'Any other crossover on Shaughnessy and Walsh?' Chris asked. 'Vines now also in the mix is a coincidence too far.'

'Yeah, I caught up on the court transcript. Not pretty.'

'Shaughnessy, who as we know was Will Vines' solicitor, kept a dossier of correspondence for his many dissenters,' Chris told her. 'Quite a bit of dissatisfaction with the guy from various quarters, as I'm sure you can imagine. Including a handwritten note, ostensibly from one of Linda Joyce's brothers.'

'A lot of name-calling and promises of karma and all that, as opposed to direct threat,' said Kennedy. 'More of 'I don't know how you sleep at night' kind of palaver. Not signed off either but was a pretty blatant rant at Shaughnessy for ensuring Vines was found not guilty.'

'You're thinking maybe someone from that family took matters into their own hands?'

'Unconfirmed as yet, but seems like the younger guy was our runner from the other day. '

'And there's certainly motive, where Vines is concerned at least. Cocky little fecker by all accounts.

'This social media stuff has the kids ruined, making them think the earth revolves around them,' Kennedy said, making a face.

'I can see why the family would be out for blood - especially when the sister took her own life after it all,' Reilly agreed. She pushed her knife and fork apart on the table to make room for the waitress to lay down her lasagne.

'Seems the media are really getting into it too,' Chris said. 'Vines in particular seems to have been universally adored.'

'Not by Suzi Cox and her coven,' she pointed out, based on something Rory had mentioned.

'Ouch, saucer of milk,' Kennedy said gleefully in the manner of one of his teenage daughters. 'I take it you're not a fan?'

'Not really. Seems like a mouthpiece who uses the so-called feminist agenda as a vehicle for her own self promotion. Apparently on some radio show the other day basically cheering Vines' demise?'

'Yep, I had my eighteen year old cursing into her phone over it.'

'Selena's a Suzi Cox fan?'

'Nope, team Vines unfortunately,' Kennedy said rolling his eyes. 'Can you believe the fecker actually got paid by fancy hotel chains and airlines to review them, free flights, hotels the whole shebang. Paid by tourist boards to review the best party pubs and clubs and what have you? No wonder kids these days don't want to work.'

Reilly couldn't help but smile. 'I may need to think about a side-hustle myself to be able to afford the rents in this town...'

'You're moving?'

'No choice,' she said, filling them in on her landlord's decision and it's precarious impact on her living situation.

'Jaysus, I don't envy you there,' Kennedy said. 'I've no idea myself if we'll ever get rid of my two, considering the cost of renting a gaff around here. They'd better get decent jobs for themselves for starters, instead of just acting the eejit on phones.'

'Like Sarah keeps telling you *Pops*, times have moved on,' Chris ribbed. 'If it were up to you, they'd be in the army or working down a coal mine.'

'Seriously though, as a parent how are you supposed to deal with that? Random Joe Soaps acting the maggot while talking through their rear end, and all the kids only lapping it up. When I try to be an 'influence' on my two they look at me like I'm shit on their shoes.' Kennedy took a sip from his newly-arrived coffee, before opening the complimentary wrapped biscuit and biting it in half. 'Tis true what they say; boys wreck your house but girls wreck your head,' he opined, before popping the other half into his mouth. Then suddenly he looked at her and paused, reddening. 'Ah Jaysus pet, I'm sorry.'

Reilly swiftly moved to dispel his (and her own) discomfort by changing the subject. 'O'Brien's not gonna be happy with all this attention though,' she said pushing her plate away, suddenly not so hungry anymore.

'Even more so if people start joining the dots and getting ahead of themselves,' Chris added eyeing her closely. 'We'll be following up with the Joyce family now and the brother in particular.'

'And I'll keep you posted if anything else jumps out in the meantime,' she told him, as Kennedy went up to the bar to pay. 'Meantime, I think I owe you a return carbonara ...' she added lightly.

Chris's face was impassive as he glanced towards the bar, as if checking his partner was out of earshot.

'Actually, there's something I do want to pick your brains about,' he said obliquely. 'I'm considering a change of scenery myself ...'

38

Lina looked out across the yard as her two girls carried feed from one of the sheds to the pig pen.

Sometimes she looked at them and couldn't believe how grown up they had become. No longer girls now, but young women.

When she and Peter had chosen to turn their backs on society, they had done so knowing they could keep their babies safe.

They hadn't had to dwell on how they could keep young *women* safe.

Now Lina lived with it everyday. The thoughts and desires, curiosity to explore, to broaden their horizons. At least that was the case with her youngest' Emmy had read so much about the world and its geography that her desire to break out had grown stronger in her, Lina could see it.

Her eldest was more content. Cici feared what lay

beyond the sanctuary they had cultivated and was more a student of the outside world; having studied the shortcomings and ways of mankind, it seemed she wanted no part in that.

Lina saw so much of Peter in her it frightened her sometimes.

In all the years since his absence, the girls had never once spoken about what had happened. They didn't miss the father he should have become, even though Lina missed the man he once was.

He had been so different to the others, her own father a mean and cruel beast that had made her young life hell.

Peter had saved her from that, but had ultimately become a victim himself.

Now she feared more regularly for the future of the girls without her when she passed away. She had always been sure the Eotwawki - End of the World as We Know It - would come soon.

Peter often spoke of the signs, even in nature he saw the earth's reaction to man as that of an organism with a parasite. It would try to rid itself of it, and they needed to be prepared for that, especially the possibility of the parasite turning on itself.

Lina wasn't sure what she believed anymore. By now the girls were more sure about the dawning of that day than she was, but that was all they'd ever known.

She had spent her life preparing them for a day she was certain was just around the corner. Now she knew she must prepare them to be able to function in the world outside their sanctum without her.

Up to now, she alone had always done supply runs for food and medical supplies; the girls only outside a couple of times for doctor or dental emergencies.

On those rare occasions, they had driven much further away from base than they needed to.

She had coached the girls to speak in their father's native tongue under the guise of being holidaymakers and they had performed excellently.

They had been awestruck by the world outside but had also been glad to get home - the dangers that their parents had foretold about a menacing threat that hung over them every second they remained outside their sanctum.

Now, Lina finished washing the dishes and saw them walking back towards the house.

Their home, their failsafe was secure.

But she knew she needed to give them the ability to walk unnoticed in the outside world too, to fetch supplies, to deal with people without drawing attention.

Now she needed to teach them how to truly survive.

39

'Why am I looking at a photo of our chief suspect on the cover of a national newspaper before we've even had a chance to interrogate him?' Inspector O'Brien demanded the following day.

Chris picked up the morning paper. 'What the ...?'

The police chief was fuming. 'Seems we have a leak. This is all we need, so please tell me we have, or are close to, picking this lad up for questioning?'

'Wasn't at lectures this week, didn't stay in campus accommodation the last few days,' Kennedy told him, looking over Chris's shoulder at the recent CCTV still-image of Ben Joyce that only they (apparently) had access to, emblazoned across the front page of the *Irish News*. 'Davis and Murphy are gone over to the parents' place this morning. Should have news shortly.'

'Let's hope so, because the Park will go ballistic over this,' their boss said gruffly, as he shooed them out the door.

'Shite.'

'You can say that again.' Chris said throwing the paper down on his desk. 'Nobody else had access to that footage, just this office.'

'What about the TV crew?'

'They said the device they gave me was the only copy. I'll check.' He pulled out his phone to see an incoming message. 'Crap. Suzi Cox is at reception. I'll bring her up, see what meeting rooms are free, will you - I'll meet you over there,' he added, heading across to the lifts.

Downstairs, he immediately spotted the outspoken journalist and female commentator waiting by the reception desk. Small in stature with a short pixie haircut and wearing a smart trouser-suit and three quarter length floral patterned coat, she was chatting to the officer on front desk duty as he approached.

'Ms Cox?'

Chris felt a limp, reluctant handshake; her small hands matching her petite frame. Suzi Cox's physical size was evidently no reflection on her reputation as a dogged and passionate campaigner for female rights.

A self proclaimed feminist, Cox had become the go-to voice in Irish media for all thing controversial.

Her 'tell it as it is' style was applauded by many and derided as inflammatory by just as many others.

The GFU cyber team had compiled a file on her online ramblings and spats, particularly those relating to their investigation - David Walsh in particular.

Chris didn't imagine her small, weak hands literally gouging out eyes, but there was something at play all the same.

This very vocal, formidable young woman had many things to say in public. Quite a few of those things in some way tied in with the actions of three men who were now dead in pretty horrific circumstances.

Had her commentary been a prompt; even a dare to Linda Joyce's brother to seek retribution?

The questioning would have to be delicate no doubt; she was here today under the guise of discussing her recent paint vandalism - though they fully intended probing her links to the Linda Joyce case and related murder victims.

Chris wondered if he should interview her alone, given Kennedy's more ... abrasive style.

'Let's find somewhere a bit quieter to chat.'

He led the way over to the lift and pressed the button as Cox walked behind, clutching her handbag.

'Will this take long Detective? I have to be on TV2 later this morning.'

'No, a few minutes is all. You've already given a statement; we're just following a line of enquiry and want to establish some facts,' he assured her, as the doors opened and he led her towards the meeting rooms where he could see Kennedy standing outside Room Three.

Chris made introductions and they all made their way inside.

'Have a seat love, do you want some tea or coffee?' Kennedy asked, as Chris tried to gauge her reaction to such a blatantly inflammatory address, but she didn't flinch.

In fact her confidence seemed to have waned a little since entering the meeting room - her initial cool demeanour replaced by a more unsettled one.

'No thanks, I'd rather just move things along if we could.'

'Rightio,' Kennedy said, throwing an eye towards Chris as he opened a file that was pretty sparse - just some photographs of her recently damaged car and paint-strewn front door along with statements from investigating officers as well as Suzi's own.

'OK, we might be covering some of the ground you've covered with the officers who responded to the incident but bear with us, we just want to make sure we have all the details,' Chris said, as she nodded her assent.

'Is there anybody that you know of that would have cause to have carried out the attacks on your car and home. I'm thinking ex lover, current lover's girlfriend that sort of thing?' Kennedy rolled in with the first question.

'I don't have an ex lover. Nothing serious anyway. I sincerely hope that isn't the angle you're looking at because it would be a waste of time, I can assure you.'

'Just important to rule it out. Nine times out of ten it's the lover scorned in these situations. OK so, no lover,' Kennedy said, pausing to write something in his notes as Suzi shuffled uncomfortably in her chair.

'Your work as a journalist, Ms Cox. It's been drawn to our attention that a few of your recent gossip columns have caused a bit of a stir.'

'Gossip columns would not be my description of my work but yes, I write about difficult social issues which invariably divides opinion.'

'Has there been any incidents in the past after you've published a ...' Kennedy seemed to be racking his brains for an alternative description.

'Article ... not physical, no. Just plenty of people willing to take a cheap shot on social media, usually trolls.'

'Not always trolls though?'

'No not always. Delicate issues and free speech always leads to heated debate - as it should.'

'Like the David Walsh episode?' Chris said relishing the opportunity to steer the conversation toward their true agenda.

'Yes, like that ... episode. Things should never

have become quite so heated, but neither of us were willing to back down at the time. We were both standing up for what we believed in.'

'And yet you felt it necessary to again reference some of that debate recently, particularly in relation to a high profile incident that went through the courts?'

'I'm not sure I understand what you are suggesting, Detective. And it's beginning to feel as though I'm under suspicion. I came here today to discuss the attacks on me - not David Walsh.' Suzi Cox's voice was wavering now as she tried to contain her concern.

Chris placed his hands on the table. 'Ms Cox, we are trying to get to the bottom of that, and indeed decide if there's any further concern of escalation. Through your social media commentary and … opinion pieces relating to the Linda Joyce trial, you've drawn a lot of attention. We are investigating the demise of Mr Walsh in relation to his engagement with you while debating the case.'

'That's all well and good, but this sounds to me like I'm guilty of some wrongdoing. All I have done is give voice to the voiceless and advocate for those who can't stand up for themselves. I've done nothing wrong, I was willing to engage a solicitor before and I still am.'

There was a steel and determination in her eyes now that was not apparent in her handshake.

She sat back in her chair and folded her arms. 'Look this conversation has drifted too far from what I was led to believe. I'm now no longer comfortable and would prefer to have a solicitor present.'

'We're done here anyway. But one piece of advice before you go Ms Cox, we are dealing with a very serious situation here. We don't know what the full picture is yet, but I think there is no denying that it may well involve some of the people and incidents that you have taken upon yourself to be the voice of. Caution is advised.' Kennedy warned, getting to his feet to match the journalist's movements.

'Thank you for your concern Detective, I'm looking forward to hearing news of you catching whoever ruined my personal property. Other that that I'd prefer if you contacted my solicitor.'

'We are not the enemy here, love, just trying to do our jobs in difficult enough circumstances without having people stirring the pot.'

'I'm certainly not your *'love'* Detective. And as far as I'm concerned there is nothing more to say.'

With that, Suzi Cox stomped out of the room, leaving the two detectives in her wake.

'Weapon,' Kennedy grunted, turning to Chris.

'Well, you seemed pretty determined to get under her skin anyway.'

'Dunno what you're talking about,' he said, all innocence.

'Do you think she got the message?'

'Judging by the 'nothing more to say' comment I hope so. I'm having conversations at home with a teenage girl whose literally gunning for that one because of her opinions on her hero. If you ask me that feckin' internet has a lot to answer for - a one way road to hate.'

40

The GFU team was slowly but surely working their way through the plethora of evidence from the current active cases.

The majority for all three crime scenes had now been processed, and they'd since begun to actively cross-reference the data.

Following Lucy's glass fragment discovery, Gary had developed a hit on the organic matter found at Sean Shaughnessy's house.

Reilly collected the files she'd been reviewing, including Will Vines' autopsy and toxicology results which made for interesting reading.

She headed for the conference room and put the files down as she looked around at the various photographs and evidence bags. 'OK where are we at?'

'Results back from the organic matter located in the boot tread marks at Sean Shaughnessy. I thought it was going to be just soil. Well, it was soil but there was a strange consistency to it. Even though it was soaked from all the rain it still retained its grittiness. So I figured I'd try to isolate it.'

'And?'

'Soon became obvious I was looking at some kind of insect husk remnants. I could make out partial wing pieces, parts of antenna and other random stuff. So I ran entomology tests and got a positive results for ... crickets.'

'Crickets. Are they indigenous?'

'No. There are several varieties of grasshopper found in this country but these seem to be from a species called Gryllodes Sigillatus or Banded cricket. A high yielding tropical species popular as a reptile feed.'

'Interesting.'

'The obvious first thing that comes to mind is a pet owner. Maybe a pet shop worker but this is where it gets interesting ...' he said glancing at Lucy to continue.

'Wet-vac remnants from the duvet and bedding from Will Vines. Without knowing about the insect thing, I got a hit on the straps for something similar.'

'Insect origins?'

'Correct.'

'OK, so we have traces of insect at two locations, as well as glass.'

'True and false at the same time,' Lucy said. 'I retested the mylar blanket and got a lot more - an overwhelmingly positive result for Gryllodes Sigillatus. Not just parts of exoskeleton, wings etc. Thanks to static, the substance recovered from that was one hundred percent positive. A hardened powder actually.'

'I'm not sure I follow ...'

'It's processed flour, ground-up crickets. I heard a lot about it recently. It's become very popular with earthy types as a sustainable alternative to traditional farming. Seems its also being used to bulk up pet food in some countries.'

Reilly scratched her head absorbing the latest developments. 'Any producers in this country?'

'There's one that raises exotics for the pet industry, but as of now nobody licensed to produce insect-derived flour in Ireland.'

'OK, Let's chase up on the pet thing. In the meantime, we can let the detectives know we have confirmed trace linking Shaughnessy and Vines. As of now, the chief suspect is Ben Joyce, brother of Linda Joyce, deceased.'

Lucy looked sad. 'I remember that case - it caused such a storm at the time.'

'Still does, it seems. One of the more vocal commentators Suzi Cox has been the centre of some attacks of late,' Reilly told her.

'What kind of attacks - physical?'

'No, property damage, paint thrown on her car, that sort of thing.'

Julius sniffed. 'Not too surprised really, she makes

a living rubbing people up the wrong way. Coming out and saying some of the things she did recently was overstepping if you ask me.'

Reilly could tell by the way the others spoke about her that Suzi Cox relished being the focus of controversy.

'The Walsh case is light though,' she pointed out. 'Only link so far is the apples, and I'd like some more. His tox screen should be back soon, hopefully that gives us something.'

'He must have been sedated in some way. Nobody is going to endure that level of mutilation without putting up a massive fight,' Gary mused.

'We'll see. Anyway we should have a suspect to run comparative DNA when they bring Joyce in.'

'Let's just hope the guy has really small feet,' Lucy said glancing up at the tread imprint left in Sean Shaughnessy's back lawn.

41

Lina watched from a distance in the hardware store, observing the girls in action on their first unaccompanied shopping expedition.

She just hoped they stuck to the script and chatted about the weather and other mundane subject matters. So far they'd drawn no suspicious glances or odd looks.

Indeed nobody - including those in the queue behind, gazes fully focused on their mobile phones while they waited in line - raised an eyebrow.

The girls bade their thanks to the assistant and walked away towards the exit, trying to minimise the grins that were threatening to go into overdrive.

Lina waited a moment longer and then followed them out to the car. They placed the bags in the back and then took their seats inside the car.

Once all the doors were shut, Emmy let out a

squeal of delight. The excitement would not have been less amongst a gang of bank robbers after a successful heist.

Cici's face in particular was flushed red as she allowed herself to breathe fully for the first time in twenty minutes.

'OK come on, calm down you two.' Lina scolded, looking around, ever watchful and protective.

She knew she would not be able to relax until they were safely at home. It would only take a moment's lapse to trip them up. A fender bender in the car park, a breakdown on the road home.

She knew making the girls more worldly-wise was important, but she also knew the stakes and risk had just increased dramatically.

'That was so much fun!' Emmy exclaimed.

'What? It was terrifying! I thought I was going to wet myself,' Cici said, eyes wide.

Lina allowed herself a little smile at her daughter's utterly different personalities, though it quickly faded as the self doubt she had been feeling lately crept back in.

Today felt a little like opening a door to the world.

And as she drove from the supermarket car park, her pre-teen girls high on their first ever independent human interaction, she felt a strong urge to slam it shut again.

42

The detectives headed into the GFU building, showing their ID to the security guard before making their way up to the labs, where they saw the usual familiar masked faces working away at various stations.

Spying their arrival, Reilly, crouched over an examination table with Lucy nodded and waved before saying something to her colleague and then heading for the door towards her office, indicating for them to follow.

'Hey,' she said by way of greeting as she dried her hands with a paper towel before tossing it into a bin.

'Don't suppose you've seen the front of the *News* today,' Kennedy said without preamble.

'No, am I missing something?'

'Seems we have a leak, a photo of our chief and only suspect from one of our very own screen grabs.'

'Damn. Is he in custody yet?'

'Nope,' Chris said before Kennedy put his foot in it and maybe started to apportion blame. 'Hopefully we get somewhere today. Davis and Murphy are on it now.'

'Is he really our guy you think?' she asked trying to gauge opinions.

'At the moment he's our best lead, unless you lot have anything that says otherwise.'

'We're still chasing up a few things. Some glass fragments from Shaughnessy's house also found at the Vines scene.'

'I got that email, but only had a chance to scan it quickly, there was traces of ... insects too?' Chris asked with a confused expression.

'Yes. But in different forms. At Shaughnessy we retrieved larger insect husks, crickets to be exact, in the boot treads. We found trace of the same insect but in a different form on the mylar blanket at Vines.'

'Different form...'

'Yes, a processed ground flour.'

'Insect flour?'

'I know, weird.' Reilly said, heading to fetch the lab report Lucy had given her before handing it to Chris.

'Lucy spoke earlier to a company that produces whole live bait and food for the exotic pet market. They don't produce flour, seems you need a government licence to do so for human consumption. They also don't keep the variety that we discovered, so unfortunately that avenue ran dry pretty quickly.'

'Wait, back up a second. Human consumption?' Kennedy repeated incredulously.

'Yeah that was my reaction too. But seems it's not actually that weird. Insects have been a huge part of the human diet in some cultures for centuries. Cheap cost of production and low environmental impact has a lot of people banking on it being a huge growth market these days. The company Lucy spoke to have applied for a licence to go into production.'

Kennedy shook his head. 'All sounds a bit hippy dippy to me. You won't catch me swapping my steak for, what was it ... cricket powder?'

Reilly laughed at the expression on Kennedy's face which was akin to that of a toddler being asked to try a new food.

And Chris realised that it had been quite some time since he'd heard that laughter.

'You obviously don't care about the planet then,' she teased.

'Don't get me started, a few farting cows is the least of our problems.'

'So how does this help, are there any other importers up north or in the UK that could be the source?' Chris asked.

'A couple, but these things are robust. They would easily survive pretty much anywhere. We'll keep digging. What do we know about the brother? Don't suppose he's an exotic pet keeper or insect farmer?'

'I think that would be lightning sticking twice,'

Chris said referring to a recent case. 'He's an engineering student. Lets hope we can find something that joins the dots.'

'Yeah,' Reilly absently looked at a copy of the offending screen grab. 'What age is he? Late teens? Unlikely profile for a killer that has carried out three very different murders with such a vast amount of flair, leaving a calling card in the process.'

'What are you thinking then?'

'I don't know, I'm just not feeling this. I guess we'll know more when you talk to him.'

'Well, he certainly has motive, not to mention he ran from a scene too,' Kennedy said matter of factly. 'And is so far MIA.'

'I wouldn't mind being an observer when you do track him down. There's a couple of questions I'd like you to throw in too, just to probe this whole thing without saying as much.'

'Shouldn't be a problem as long as we *do* get him in,' Chris shrugged. 'So, apples, glass and insects. Anything useful in the toxicology?'

'Actually that's the main reason I wanted you to call today rather than discuss over the phone. Tox screen for Vines and Walsh both showed some interesting results. Taking Walsh first up; the biggest piece of the puzzle from the get-go was how the attacker managed to do what they did, right?'

'You mean why he didn't resist?'

'Yes, we always assumed he was subdued in some manner, probably chemically, but initial autopsy findings didn't offer much. The tox report offers something a little more useful found in that drink pack he was carrying; traces of atropine, scopolamine and hyoscyamine.'

'Sedatives?' Chris asked.

'Potentially, but given the amounts found and the known rate of dissipation, especially postmortem we can safely say that whatever was administered was a potent one.'

'So what are you thinking?'

'Two things, whoever administered it was at close enough range to do so. No injection wounds were found, though some areas of his body and indeed the hydration pack itself, was damaged from him stumbling through the briars etc, so it's impossible to say for sure. Secondly, I suspect the dosage maybe wasn't intended as a sedative but rather a poison. Either way, whoever gave it to him couldn't have known what effect it would have.'

'So this poison, is it easy to access?'

'Without a comparative sample, it's impossible to know exactly what it was. Tropane alkaloids are naturally occurring, typically of plant origin.'

'So you think Walsh wasn't supposed to wake up and go walkabout after all?'

'Impossible to know. Unless you'd specifically tested the dosage to gauge potency on the intended subject, you'd really only be guessing. Quick and easy deaths don't seem to be a theme here, but then again leaving a victim to wander around and potentially survive doesn't seem to fit the MO either.'

'OK, if we can get Joyce to willingly supply a DNA sample we might be able to cross-reference with whatever you've got here. And get Spud or Sarah to run his phone records - see if we can get any pings for the locations and times we're looking at,' Chris said, as Lucy walked into the room.

'Thought I might as well bring these to your attention while you're here,' she said holding up another report. 'The other result is in relation to the glasses at Vines' place. We assumed the alcohol was vodka or gin since it was clear, but that doesn't seem to be the case,' Lucy said glancing down at the results.

'Do we know what it was?' Chris asked.

'Poitín. Almost 65% ABV - so very potent.'

'Poitín?' Reilly repeated.

'I think you'd be more familiar with the term moonshine,' Chris said.

'Yeah, was all the rage years ago, you'd often hear tales of people getting some from 'a fella' down the country. My uncles used to keep some and swore t'was a cure for everything.' Kennedy said fondly.

'So I'm guessing it's illegal here too.'

'The homemade variety is anyway, though to be honest you don't hear much about it anymore. Far easier to go Lidl and buy a couple of bottles of cheap plonk. There was a counterfeiting ring bust last year where an eastern European gang were distilling a form and bottling it unbranded to sell cheap to pubs,' Chris said.

'Those generally use barley, whereas our analysis seems to indicate what was in Vines' apartment was derived from more traditional ingredients - such as potatoes and molasses,' Lucy pointed out.

'Does that help us in any way though?'

'I'm not sure. What about fingerprints on the glasses?' Chris asked, as he leaned back against Reilly's desk taking the weight off his aching legs.

'Both pristine, no prints. Have to assume they were wiped,' she offered. 'We're not dealing with a clueless vigilante here. Whoever is responsible is as meticulous as they are ballsy. Just have to hope they've made a mistake somewhere.'

'Well, I can't think of any other reason Ben Joyce bolted outside Vines' apartment that time other than the fact he had something to hide.' Chris said, as he pulled his phone from his pocket and answered it.

The words he used when speaking to the person on the other end of the line quickly gave away the subject matter.

'We have him?' Kennedy asked as he slipped his phone back in his pocket.

'Yep, Spud and Sarah just picked him up back at DCU campus dorm.'

'Nice one.'

'They're going to have a quick chat, while we call the parents and get the family's legal representative on standby. If we need more time we can always slap in a charge for resisting arrest.'

'Sounds good to me. I just hope he's our guy. If he isn't and it's discovered that a leak leading to his picture and speculation in the press has come from us, his solicitor will have a field day...' Kennedy grumbled. 'And someone is in deep shit.'

43

Back at the station, the detectives sat anxiously at their desks, half studying test results and address details for insect importers in the UK.

The imminent arrival of their chief - in fact only - suspect, was making concentration difficult.

Chris started to go through some mail that had been piling up, when one envelope in particular caught his attention.

Ripping open the seal, he took the neatly folded page out and started to read; the words triggering a range of different emotions.

Phrases like '*Delighted to offer*' and '*congratulations*' danced across the page.

In the midst of the investigation, he had pretty much put his promotion application to the back of his mind, apart from briefly dancing around the idea to Reilly in the pub the other day, before Kennedy's reappearance had cut short any further conversation.

There were some big decisions to be made now though. The magnitude of the current case meant that he could probably kick the can down the road for a little while at least; the powers that be understanding the need for resolution without distraction.

But he was fast running out of time to say something to Kennedy before the grapevine did the job for him.

'Hey,' the big man said, tossing a scrunched up piece of paper in his direction. 'You're worse than one of my two at home lately, off in dreamland all the time. Everything all right?'

Inwardly Chris cursed the timing; this particular minute wasn't right to broach the subject either - especially at such a pivotal moment in the investigation so far.

'Sorry, just working out some angles for the Joyce interview.'

'Don't lead with the incident outside Vines' apartment anyway, lets just dance a bit first, get a sense of his attitude. Reilly still coming?'

'Think so. She's always more interested in seeing suspects in the flesh, you know her and her Spidey sense.'

'Yeah, she doesn't seem sold on Joyce though.'

'I got that feeling too,' Chris said, as his phone beeped to herald a text from Sarah announcing their arrival. 'They're downstairs,' he told Kennedy, having asked her to bring the suspect up.

'This should be interesting,' the other man said, getting to his feet and grabbing a thick bunch of files, many completely unrelated to the case, but thick enough to elicit a sense of discomfort in the interviewee.

As they walked to the interview rooms, Sarah and Spud exited the lift with Ben Joyce following behind, escorted by a middle-aged rotund suit the detectives deduced was the family solicitor.

Chris noted that the legal rep looked more nervous than the young man he accompanied. Probably more used to handling property deeds and family wills than potential high profile multiple murder cases.

Not that he was complaining. Somebody of Sean Shaughnessy's ilk would have been far less conducive to a productive first interview.

Spud showed the two men into the interview room and made enquiries about refreshments which were politely declined, before heading back out to where Chris and Kennedy were standing with Sarah.

'He's been quiet, not very talkative - only to give the minimum feedback. Didn't say a word in the car either,' Murphy said.

'Seems like the cogs are turning but he's not asking us any questions. The father was waiting downstairs when we came in just now, and definitely become more emotional when they greeted each other,' Sarah confirmed.

'He's lightweight enough; what would you say; five-six, five-seven?'

'Might be lightweight but he had no problem getting away from you down at Docklands,' Spud jibed.

'The one who's talking. Anything else interesting pop up when you caught up with him?'

'Like I said, seems cool enough. I'd expect a guy of his age to be a bit more full of bravado.'

'You think the thing in the paper this morning tipped him off?'

'I'm not sure if he'd have seen it, more likely one of his mates copped it and alerted him. Have a chat and see what you think. I know if I was innocent and my face was smeared across the media pointing the finger, I'd be a lot more pissed off than this fella is.'

They left the others and headed for the interview room, Chris leading the introductions.

'OK Ben, thanks for coming in to help us out. I trust the other detectives gave you a rundown of why you're here?' he began, as he and Kennedy took seats opposite the two men.

Before Ben had a chance to answer, his solicitor piped up.

'Good afternoon detectives. Yes we've had a brief run-through, but before we begin I'd like it noted on record our anger and upset at the fact my client has been slandered and defamed in traditional media due to the despicably unprofessional, if not tactical, leak of his details.'

'Noted Mr Hobbs. That was an unfortunate incident which we're currently looking into.'

'That's well and good for you to say Detective, but let me tell you this, I have known and worked with Ben and his family for decades. They are not people to engage in the kind of depravity those newspaper reports were alluding to.' The solicitor had quickly shaken off his early demeanour and seemed far spikier than was first apparent.

'As I said, your points are noted. We simply want to have a quick chat for now if that's OK?'

Ben looked at the solicitor who gave a single nod, granting his agreement to allow the interview to proceed.

'Thank you,' Kennedy opened the top file of his thick pile looking up just in time to see the suspect's Adams apple bounce in his throat as he swallowed hard. 'Ben. Are you familiar with a man named Sean Shaughnessy?'

'Of course,' he said with a shrug, as if it was obvious.

'What about David Walsh?'

'I know of him, read some of his stuff.'

'You've never met him personally?'

'No.'

'We know you're familiar with William Vines though, yes?'

Ben swallowed hard and looked at his solicitor who nodded discreetly.

'Yes.'

'Did you know him personally?'

'More that I knew *of* him. Far more than I ever wanted to.'

'Ben, we are aware of what happened with your sister, and are truly sorry....' He looked indifferent, hard to read. 'These other men, you've probably seen the recent news coverage, and may be aware that they were all involved in some way with your sister's case. Sean Shaughnessy acted as William Vines' legal counsel and David Walsh was a prominent reporter who also wrote extensively about the trial.'

'Walsh and Vines were best buds. If you've been investigating, you'd know that much,' Ben said, sitting back in his seat.

'We know he defended William Vines' character in the media certainly. We also know he became embroiled with some intense public spats whereupon he was accused of victim-blaming for his opinions.'

'Sounds like you know everything already then, so what do you need me for?'

'Just trying to get the full picture. We are also aware that you yourself made some ... angry public accusations in the aftermath of the court proceedings.'

'Have you got sisters?' Ben asked, sitting forward.

'Yes two,' Kennedy replied.

'Were either of them ever attacked and had their reputations publicly dragged through the mud, turned into a laughing stock - a fucking *hashtag* - just for trying to seek justice?' Ben's hands trembled and his voice took on a higher pitch as his anger constricted his throat. 'To the point that they no longer wanted to live?'

He sat back in his chair, and just as Hobbs was about to intervene and seek to take a moment, Ben spoke again. 'I know what you're getting at; these pricks are dead, so you automatically think it was me because of my sister. Well, you're barking up the wrong tree.'

Chris looked at him for a moment and then to Kennedy, both knowing that the time was right.

'You know we've met before Ben, yes?' he asked, causing the kid to pause for thought before shrugging yet again.

'Outside William Vines' apartment building in the Docklands last week - you saw me approach, and you ran.'

'Hold on there, Detective, Ben you don't need to answer that.'

'Come on Mr Hobbs, that picture in the newspaper you took such offence to … it was taken outside the apartment, a screen grab from video footage which clearly shows Ben here running from the scene of a crime.'

'Well then Detectives, this interview was entirely a courtesy. Unless you are pressing charges, my client and I are leaving,' the solicitor said, getting to his feet.

'Hold on, I've nothing to hide here,' Ben's voice now grew angry. 'This is a joke right? I knew that this would happen - thats why I bolted. You haven't a bloody clue, do you? Yes I was there....'

'Ben, as your solicitor I think it's best we discuss this further in private before you continue,' Hobbs said, but Ben couldn't be stopped as his anger bubbled over.

'Yes I was happy that dickhead was gone. The other two I couldn't care less about, but I enjoyed watching all those fake, grieving, idiot followers of his with their mock tears. They hadn't a clue what he really was. For the first time since my sister was let down by the likes of you two, for the first time since she was driven to take her own life I felt ... peace. I didn't kill anyone but I'll lose no sleep over that piece of shit.'

Ben stood up to join his solicitor, who wore a look of panic not knowing what his client was going to say next or if he would be capable of stopping him.

'Are we finished here, Detectives?' Hobbs asked.

'No, I'm afraid not. Ben Joyce I'm detaining you under section 4 of the Criminal Justice Act 1997. You are not obliged to say anything unless you wish to do so, but whatever you say will be taken down in writing and may be given in evidence.'

Ben slumped back down into his seat reeling off several more expletives.

'Here is the charge sheet,' Chris said, sliding the document across the table and proceeding to read out the charges set and giving them time to respond before making a note of each response.

He then gave details of secured warrants to search Ben's student accommodation and family home in relation to the charges, before leaving the two men alone to discuss next procedures.

Once outside, they were met by Sarah and a newly-arrived Reilly.

'How'd it go?' the female detective asked.

'Well, he didn't break down and confess, although he does admit to running from the scene at Vines' place.'

'Kind of hard to deny with the photo. Not to mention the prints lifted from the bike lock,' Reilly offered. 'What's your gut tell you, though?'

'He has a lot of anger, which is understandable. Motive too, obviously. He's not a big guy, but then again I don't suppose he needed to be.'

'Yep,' added Kennedy. 'Doesn't exactly have clown feet either - I'm not the best at judging these things, but even I know those imprints don't fit.'

'That's your head, what does your gut tell you?'

'Reilly, you do know I've spent a lifetime trying to think with my head rather than my gut, grand and all that it is,' he shot back, fondly patting his large girth.

'In the meantime, let's nail down the phone records - see if we can place Joyce at or near any of the other scenes in the correct time frame,' Chris said. 'We can only hold him for twenty-four hours so better get moving. Reilly, we'll need your crew to do a sweep of his place to see if there is anything to nail him.'

Sarah nodded. 'Let's just hope we get something. If we don't, it's going to look pretty bad. Some of the publicity around his sister's case wasn't too kind to us either. If we have an unjustified detainment following on from that leaked photo ...'

'Some progress on the leak too it seems,' Reilly said glancing at a sheet of paper she'd brought with her. 'Rory narrowed down the timeline. The picture first appeared on social media, and spread wide and far there pretty quickly. Contact details for the original poster too,' she murmured, handing the sheet to Chris who looked at it briefly before passing it to Kennedy.

Whereupon studying its contents, the blood drained from his partner's face.

44

'Where's he off to in such a rush?' Reilly asked, when Kennedy promptly grabbed his coat and hurried away.

'Said something about a problem at home,' Chris told her.

'Oh, hope nothing serious.'

'So, what do you reckon on Joyce? You're honestly not keen?'

'He has motive obviously. But it begs the question, why so elaborate? Electrocution, roasting, eye gouging - seems way over the top, even if he is a grieving brother. And what's the significance of the apples?'

'I hear you, but maybe once the warrants come through and we get the team in place to comb through his stuff, we might find more.'

'I'm just not sure Chris, even the whole running away that time, I'm just not feeling it.'

'I'm keeping an open mind on it too, but since we've little else to go on at the minute, I don't have much of a choice.' Then he paused. 'Anyway, while you're here, do you have time for a cuppa? Like I said the other day, there's something I'd like to run by you - something ... unrelated to all of this.'

'Damn. I would but I need to head to the airport to pick up Daniel.'

'Forrest's in town?'

'Yes. Lecturing in Trinity, or so he says.' She made a face.

'Sure you're OK about seeing him?' he asked, and again she marvelled at how easily he could read her.

'It's fine, he's only here for the weekend. But hey, why don't you come over anyway - Sunday, maybe?'

'No, it's grand, honestly. It can wait.'

'I mean it. I owe you dinner, remember.'

'Sure we'll see how it goes.'

And as she headed for the exit, Reilly got the sense that once again, she had let Chris down.

KENNEDY SLAMMED the car door shut and moved towards his front door quicker than he'd done in years.

'Hi love, you're home very early - everything all right?' Josie asked.

'No, it's not actually. Are the girls here?'

'Julie's at swimming, Selena's upstairs - why what's wrong?' his wife pressed, worried.

'I'll fill you in later,' he muttered angrily, making a beeline for the stairs.

'Selena, you in there?' He rapped on his eldest's bedroom door, his level of anger not high enough to risk walking straight into her bedroom without knocking. He knew the ramifications for that wouldn't be worth the risk no matter the situation.

'Yeah.'

'Can you come out here please?'

'In a minute.'

'*Now,*' he roared.

'Alright, alright ...' A deep sigh, and then he could hear footsteps stomping towards the door and the latch being flicked.

Selena's face appeared and her mouth moved, about to give a typical 'what's the big deal' attitude, but then just as quickly she snapped it shut upon seeing her father's crimson completion and angry gaze.

'Can you explain this?' He thrust a sheet of paper at her as Josie moved into position behind, sensing a referee might be required.

'Umm no ...what's that all about?'

'You tell me. Your friend Emily - that's her Twitter name, isn't it?'

'Yes.'

'Recognise this?' He thrust a second sheet at her and upon seeing the photo, Selena's face dropped.

'Oh.'

As did her father's insides.

'Oh....*Oh* ... that's all you've got to say?'

'OK, what the hell is going on here - will somebody please tell me?' Josie demanded.

'Why don't you tell your mother, cos I'm all ears myself. I think I know what's happened, but in the interest of fairness, I'd love to hear your version.'

His daughter looked very sheepish as she backed into the room and sat on the edge of her bed, eyes cast down as her parents moved out of the confines of the hallway into her bedroom.

'Sorry.'

'Sorry doesn't cut it. Do you know how much hassle this is going to cause? I'll be in serious trouble over this, do you understand?'

'*You're* in trouble, hold on, can somebody please explain to me why you'd be in trouble because of Emily?' Josie was getting more confused by the second.

Kennedy snatched the pieces of paper from Selena and handed them to his wife.

'That lad in that photo happens to be our chief suspect in the current investigation that's been causing me sleepless nights. The photo was posted via Emily's Twitter account and shared to her silly little Willy Vines' fan club before going all over the place. Using another feckin' hashtag 'mostwanted'. *Before* we got to arrest the guy.'

'But what has that got to do with Selena?'

'Bloody hell Josie, Emily's father isn't one of the chief investigators in the case. Where do you think the photo came from ... look, you can clearly see it was snapped in the study downstairs.'

Her face paled as she turned to her daughter. 'Tell me you didn't ...'

'I'm really sorry ... I didn't really think...'

'You can say that again. Lookit, I'm going to try and sort this out - see if I can save myself *and* you from a shit-load of trouble. And in the meantime, you're grounded.'

'Dad, I'm seventeen. You can't ground me.'

'You know what - you're right. Let me put it another way then. I don't want you putting a foot outside this house, or talking to your buddies online till I figure out how to sort this shit-show. If you have a problem with that, then you're free to leave.'

'*Pete* ...' Josie was horrified.

'I mean it, love. This is a big deal. A huge overstep. And if it ends up costing us this case, then a social media ban will be the very least of her worries.'

45

s Chris headed back to his desk, Sarah called him over.

'What's up?'

'Just this whole Suzi Cox thing ...'

'What about her? Anything on the vandalism?'

'Just some CCTV footage from the TV station car park. Not great, a bit too dark but you can clearly see a figure walking past and discreetly tossing the paint at it.'

'Any chance we can figure Joyce for that too?' he asked, clutching at straws. 'Got to be male anyway, seems most women idolize her as some kind of feminist freedom fighter.'

Sarah made a face. 'Well, I'm not most women and she certainly doesn't speak for me - more shit-stirrer than feminist to my mind. And I don't think many of Will Vines' rabid female following would be fans either.'

'So what are you thinking?' he asked, glancing at her monitor whereupon Cox's social media feed was displayed.

'There seems to be a group of what I'd describe as hardcore feminists coming out in defence and support of Suzi and her comments, articles and online tussles - particularly anything to do with Vines. This one in particular caught my eye.'

Sarah duly clicked on some links and brought up the relevant account, which made his eyes widen.

The profile image was starkly familiar; a classic painting of a naked woman standing in front of a tree holding an apple. The account handle was listed as @ForbiddenFruit.

Chris scanned the feed as Sarah scrolled down. A series of tweets and retweets relating to the general mistreatment of women and multiple tales of male comeuppance.

'Is Suzi Cox heavily involved with this group do you know?'

'Hard to tell, but she's certainly a fan anyway. They seem to repeatedly reshare and amplify each other's posts, and there's a lot of reciprocal admiration. Though this in particular is what caught my attention,' Sarah added, as she brought up a new window; a retweet of a news article about Vines' murder, the only commentary an emoji of an old-fashioned weighing scales.

'The scales of justice?' Chris ventured.

'But even more interestingly…' Sarah clicked on a

tab to open yet another account. 'Liked and reshared at the time by none other than ... Ben Joyce.'

He looked at her. 'OK. We need to find out more about this Forbidden Fruit thing, and exactly who's behind it.'

'Already on it.'

'Nice one Sarah, give me a shout once you find anything.'

He headed onwards to his desk, his mind racing.

Ben Joyce certainly had motive. But if he hadn't carried out those attacks himself, could he have been the poster boy for some kind of vigilante feminist mission?

He felt there was something to it, but he just couldn't fit the pieces together yet and his mind swirled with all the various permutations as he worked.

An hour or so later, Kennedy returned. 'What did I miss?'

'Where did you fly off to in such a rush. Everything OK?'

'Not really. I found the leak.'

'What - who?'

'Selena.'

'Wait, what ... as in *your* Selena?'

He nodded.

'How?'

'All this Vines fan club bullshit. I'd been researching the Joyce kid at home - remember when I phoned you about that news clip? I was comparing the screen grab to the TV footage at the time, and printed out some stuff on the family printer. Selena obviously came across it, took a snap of the pic on her phone and shared it with a friend - who shared it with the feckin' world.'

'Shit.'

'You could say that.'

'What are you going to do?'

'I'll have to let the boss man know, I suppose. To think I was going around shouting blue murder and pointing the finger, and I was to blame all the time.'

'Well, you weren't exactly to blame. We can spin it to O'Brien that Selena made an innocent mistake, she didn't know its significance or importance. She's only young after all.'

'She should know better. And it doesn't reflect well.'

'I wouldn't sweat it, and as it turns out it played no bearing really, since we got him in right after.'

'Yeah, but what if he's innocent? We'll have our asses sued off us.'

'I wouldn't worry just yet. GFU's going to sweep his place now - we'll know pretty quick if there's any meat on the bones. In the meantime, Sarah's onto something too. For once, all that desperation to share and comment might just play in our favour.'

46

Reilly's thoughts were on autopilot as she drove to the airport, having since agreed to pick Daniel up from his incoming flight and drop him to his city centre hotel.

She figured it would be a far more easygoing encounter than meeting for dinner, plus have a getaway plan on standby if the conversation went awry or got too ... intense.

Lately, things seemed to be changing at an unstoppable pace. It seemed like only yesterday that she'd been seriously considering moving back to the US to raise a child alongside Daniel's son.

While it had been pretty clear there was no future for her and Todd, ultimately her choice to remain here had been for many reasons; the people she worked with, making a real difference on the job.

But wasn't it mostly, albeit subconsciously, because of Chris? Because there was no doubt that she was missing home these days, far more than ever before.

She had initially come here for a specific reason, but since then, her dad had got better and moved on - was actually thriving these days. Whereas now she seemed to be the one stuck in an endless loop of self-destruction.

Mike had been urging her to come home too, insisting she should be with family at such a difficult time.

But no, Reilly had once again stuck to her guns, convinced that the job would as always, be her saviour.

Though she had to admit that this time, it wasn't working.

While of course she was fully immersed in this investigation, she got the sense that she was overlooking certain elements, and it was Lucy who was making the faster connections and chasing the right avenues these days.

Whereas she herself was feeling a little behind the curve. Which for Reilly, was a complete revelation.

Though she supposed, also testament to just how good the GFU team was that they didn't seem to need her anymore.

But if work didn't need her, and it was no longer the lifesaver it used to be, then ... what else was there?

After so much time in law enforcement, there

was little doubt she needed a change, and while the very last thing Reilly would have chosen was motherhood, she'd been at least willing to see where that went.

As Chris used to say, it would be a brand new adventure.

But clearly that avenue was not the right one for her either, since it was very quickly closed to her too.

And now, instead of driving to the airport to pick up her child's grandfather, she was instead facing what she knew would be a highly uncomfortable conversation with someone she cared deeply about.

Reilly shook her head in disbelief as she pulled into the airport short term car park, having no real memory of the journey she'd been so lost in her own thoughts.

Parking the car, she made her way inside the terminal building and checked the screens for Daniel's flight, realising that it had already touched down.

In the arrivals hall, she studied the typical array of characters making their way through the white sliding doors as she waited.

Sharply-dressed business people travelling light and trying to escape the airport as quickly as possible. The more casually dressed, sun-kissed holidaymakers mourning a return to normality. Returning emigrant families being greeted by excited relations, tired kids awkwardly giving reluctant embraces to people they barely knew.

Until finally, a lone distinguished figure who'd played such a major role in her life.

She waved to Daniel as he navigated his luggage trolley to avoid severing somebody achilles. Even though he'd flown via the UK where he'd also been lecturing at Oxford, he still had that unmistakable Floridian glow that put her in the mind of sun, sea and sand.

And right then Reilly felt such a longing for home that it was almost palpable.

The two embraced with more affection than some of the extended families she'd witnessed while waiting and she hugged Daniel tight, the fact that they'd come so close to indeed being family not lost on her.

And all of a sudden, in the warmth of her old friend and mentor's embrace, the dam of emotions she'd been holding back for so long seemed to crack.

And Reilly finally allowed herself to feel ... something.

47

'Why do you always have to draw so much attention to yourself?' Cici scolded her sister as they crossed the car park, having this time visited a different hardware store for supplies.

'You're just jealous that he was talking to me,' Emmy taunted.

'Jealous ...Why the hell would I be jealous of some creepy man?'

'Because he was flirting with me, not you.'

'Flies find pig-shit attractive too. Remember Mama told us not to attract attention.'

'Oh, don't be such a stick in the mud. Don't you ever get tired of the same old scary stories day in day out? I know what she says, but people on the outside don't seem that bad to me.'

'You know as well as I do what's at stake,' her elder sister scolded, opening the car door. 'The minute you start to feel that way, the second you let your guard down....'

'Guard down?' their mother enquired, as both girls fastened their seat belts.

'Emmy was drawing attention to herself again.'

'I was not. Us two standing there all wide-eyed and mute draws more attention. I was just trying to be *normal*. If somebody asks me a question I'm not going to stare at my shoes. Cici acts like a deer in the headlights - people think she's weird.'

'That's enough.' Lina said, turning on the ignition. 'We're well-stocked up now and once the colony starts to thrive we'll have less need for outside interaction.' She glanced at the cardboard box filled with clear plastic containers, and a few small square foil packets.

'How many did you get?'

'Ten, and the man made some stupid joke about preparing for the apocalypse.' Emmy replied gruffly, still annoyed at her sister. 'So I had to do something.'

48

'Ready for your field trip?'

'Don't tell me it's another murder, I don't know if we can handle it,' Gary groaned.

'Thankfully not, just need to run the rule under the suspect's digs,' Reilly replied, relieved herself that their workload was not being increased just when they'd started to make some headway.

And that last night's conversation with Daniel had been a lot easier than she'd anticipated. Despite her outburst of emotion at the airport, they'd chatted easily in the car on the way to his hotel, merely discussing this latest case - which she guessed was his way of helping her regain her equilibrium.

Work demands in advance of another busy day today had also allowed her to cry off on dinner when dropping him off at the Westbury, and promised to catch up with him properly after his lecture.

'How's all shaping up anyway?' Lucy asked now.

'Detectives are chasing down phone records and checking out Ben Joyce's alibi. Today, we need to be thorough and we can't afford to miss anything. If we can put Joyce at the scene, then we're golden.'

As the others went to gather up their gear and head off, Reilly's phone buzzed in her pocket. Pulling it out she saw Chris's number.

'Hey.'

'Can you talk?'

'Sure.'

'A couple of developments before you head out. One is William Vines' social media records. Vines was routinely pictured with various figures from the Irish media from the time to time - no surprise given his celeb status. But Sarah tracked down a shot of him with someone unexpected, given her public views,' Chris said dramatically, pausing to make sure he had her attention. 'Suzi Cox.'

'The journo again?'

'Yep. Papped with him at a media event a month or so after the trial.'

'But wasn't she famously damning about Vines' involvement in all that?'

'Absolutely. Sarah's also uncovered some suspect online interactions of hers with the social media handle @ForbiddenFruit; a very vocal voice with a distinct anti-male platform. The profile page alone is compelling to say the least - I've just sent you a link.'

Reilly moved to the desktop and logged in,

accessing her email. As the page opened, the background image on the account in question was anything but background. Eve in the garden of Eden holding the forbidden fruit. An apple.

'You still there?'

'All this is way too close to the bone to be coincidence surely?' she muttered, as she read through pages and pages of what could only be described as extreme feminist propaganda.

'Yep. Turns out it wasn't just Suzi Cox who had routine interactions with this particular account though. Ben Joyce was also a bit of a cheerleader.'

Her mind raced. 'So what's the plan?'

'We're bringing Suzi Cox back in, along with the actual person behind that Forbidden Fruit thing. In our last interview, Cox also had ample opportunity to reveal a closer association with Ben Joyce himself, yet chose not to. We need to know why.'

'Considering some of that stuff involving David Walsh - she doesn't seem the type to keep things low key, in fact Ms Cox seems to be the quintessential over-sharer.'

'Agreed.'

'OK, let me know if anything in particular you need from us here, and I'll update you on any preliminary findings from Joyce's place.'

'We're getting close Reilly, I can feel it in my bones,' Chris said, his enthusiasm evident.

'Lets hope so.'

Hanging up, she continued to scroll through the Forbidden Fruit social media feed.

The world truly was changing; and at such a rapid pace that it was almost frightening.

Everyone now had the medium to disseminate their thoughts, agenda, and own version of the truth - to radicalise and be radicalised, all from a tiny device in their pocket.

And in Reilly's world, a mix of strong opinions and high emotion pretty much always made for a toxic result.

49

Lucy and Gary made the short journey to Dublin City University, their discussions ranging from the current case to personal plans for the weekend.

As they approached the entrance to the campus student apartment block, they could see two squad cars with officers standing on the grass verge chatting.

Gary pulled the van in behind them and they both got out.

'Morning folks,' the officer said in a cheery manner. 'We have the warrant ready, and had somebody from the management company here to open up so it's all ready to go.'

'Great, thanks. We'll just get set up and you can lead the way.'

The two duly grabbed their kitbags and equipment from the van, after putting on their dust suits and shoe coverings.

The officer lead them up a pedestrian pathway to a set of timber and glass double doors with a panel of door buzzers on one side, and a large double row of letterboxes on the other. Once inside, they went up one flight of stairs and along a landing.

Further up the corridor, another officer was standing sentry outside Ben Joyce's room. He acknowledged them and opened the door as they placed their equipment on the floor before fully suiting up and making their way inside.

Going through the narrow, dark hallway they emerged into an open plan living room/kitchen. Though compact, there was ample space and storage even though it was pretty messy with drink cans, half full ashtrays and empty pizza boxes scattered across the small kitchen table. Typical student digs.

'Bit of a whiff in here,' Gary said now regretting not wearing a face mask given they were looking for comparative evidence, as opposed to working a crime scene.

'Yeah, smells like a mouldy old bin,' Lucy agreed wrinkling her nose. 'Any chance you'd do the bedroom? I don't fancy picking through this guy's bedclothes.'

'Cheers,' Gary groaned, picking up his bag and making his way through the bedroom door.

Lucy could see the unmade bed and dirty

clothing strewn across the floor as she walked past the doorway.

She removed the camera and attached a wide angled lens before proceeding to document the living room area, followed by the kitchen. Opening the kitchen cupboards, she photographed the contents before finishing up in the hallway, routinely cataloguing everything as she went, and trying to keep an open mind, while also keeping an eye out for anything more obvious.

Once finished, she popped her head into the bedroom where Gary was on his hands and knees combing through the carpet on what little clear spaces there were.

Nice.

'I'll leave this here for when you're ready,' she told him, placing the camera just inside the door. She glanced in disgust at the bed, noting the well-stained sheets that no doubt would give them ample opportunity to sample various bodily fluids.

She then started to work her way through everything for a second time, this time methodically bagging and labelling several pieces of what she hoped might prove to be useful.

Lucy knew if she could match something from this apartment with trace they already had, they were onto something.

But she also knew that the clock was ticking, and that in order to charge Joyce, the detectives needed something to nail him with - and fast.

Having bagged and labelled several samples, she moved back to the kitchen. The sink was unsurprisingly full of dirty dishes, and she opened the storage area underneath to discover the cause of the overriding pungent odour - an overflowing rubbish bin.

The ripe stench up-close hit her square in the nose, and she reeled back, allowing it to subside a little as she subconsciously raised the back of her gloved hand to her nose.

She gently lifted out the overflowing swing bin, recalling her own college days when she had shared a house with five others.

The boys had been pigs, too used to having Mammy tidy up after them. The bin was often the very thing that caused arguments. According to the lads, if you could fit more in it wasn't full, so therefore didn't need to be emptied.

For a long time she had struggled to find independence from her parents after the tragic disappearance of her sister. When she did finally start to find her own place in the world, Lucy realised that being a control freak was just in her nature.

She went to her kit bag and removed a fresh refuse sack from a roll. Then taking plastic tweezers, began the arduous task of sifting through items from the bin and placing them in the sack - just in case. She continued to transfer the bin's contents piece by piece, and as she got closer to the bottom, Gary stuck his head over the countertop.

'How're we doin' here?'

'Not a lot, you?'

'Yep.' He triumphantly held up a clear plastic bag that looked to contain weed. But while it was something, Lucy figured it was also par for the course in student digs, so she wasn't going to get too excited.

'Plenty to cross-reference from the bedroom to be fair. There's an iPad in there; should we bag that too?'

'Needs a special access request, I think. And we don't have one.'

'Think that's us nearly done then,' Gary said, wrinkling his nose at the stench.

'Get the vac and do the mat inside the front door,' she suggested, as she finished her fruitless search of the putrid rubbish, save for an empty glass bottle with a handwritten label. 'There's a storage cupboard in the hall too that I haven't had a chance to get to yet.'

Gary duly took out the small but powerful hand vacuum they used to sift through smaller-sized trace.

A little later, Lucy packed away her slim pickings and her gear before making her way out to the hall to inspect the cupboard.

Opening back the double doors, she spied a couple of coats and jackets hanging up, some toilet rolls in a half-used multipack, plus a sweeping brush and dustpan.

The dustpan was one of those with a knee-high handle and small brush that clips into it to save a person having to squat down. In typical lazy male student fashion, the pan had been used to clean up something, then placed back in the cupboard without being emptied.

Nice one ...

Lucy crouched down and took a sample of the dirt which actually looked more like a spillage of some kind. As she rose to her feet, she saw something sticking out from behind a thick winter coat.

Reilly was often commended for her nose; her weirdly perceptive sense of smell. Whereas Lucy's party-piece was quickly becoming colour, or rather her ability to compare and match particular shades.

Years of being a dedicated follower of fashion had finally counted for something other than maxed-out credit cards.

Lucy pulled the coat back to get a better look at what had caught her attention and she peered closer, examining it between her gloved fingers.

Gotcha.

50

'Are they both here?' Chris asked, as he joined Kennedy outside the interview rooms.

'Yep, what way do you want to do this?'

'Let's start off with Cox and then move onto ...' He searched the piece of paper for the other name, 'Harris.'

'Can you fill me in again? This whole business with Selena has me out of the loop a bit. You're thinking these two might be in cahoots for this?'

'Not sure yet, though they're indeed in cahoots in some shape or form, and not just in the virtual world either. Sarah, online whizz-kid that she is, has since found Cox and Harris pictured together at the vigil held for Linda Joyce after she passed away. We don't know if Harris had anything much to do with that case as such. But there's *definitely* more to Ms Cox than meets the eye. Interesting to see if it has anything to do with apples...'

The detectives walked into the first interview room where Suzi Cox, this time accompanied by her solicitor, was waiting.

Both looked ready and willing to cross swords.

'Morning ladies,' Chris greeted smoothly. The two nodded but didn't return a vocal greeting.

'OK, let's get to it,' Kennedy began, having set up the recording equipment and read the necessary preceding statements. 'Ms Cox, can you outline for us your relationship with the Joyce family?'

Suzi sat forward, glancing at her solicitor who nodded permission to answer the question.

'I know the family from Linda Joyce's court case, which I attended in a journalist capacity.'

'The trial concerning the accusations against William Vines - correct?'

'Well, it was ultimately more of an accusation against Linda Joyce, but yes, that's the one,' Suzi confirmed tersely.

'Was your relationship with the Joyce family of a professional nature would you say?'

'Initially, yes.'

'It moved to a more personal one after the trial?'

'Yes, it's no secret that I'm involved with SASI, Sexual Assault Survivors Ireland. And Linda came to this group to avail of its services.'

'How did she come to know of the group?'

'She was approached online by a fellow member who introduced her to us.'

'And that fellow member was....?'

'Sorry Detective, I'm just not sure how this has any relevance,' Suzi's solicitor interjected.

'Look, let's be clear, there is no obligation to answer any of our questions here today. But there are some elements from our perspective that need clarifying in relation to the demise of three men associated with this particular case. You can help us out willingly, or we can do it under official caution.'

'I had nothing to do with what happened to those!' Suzi cried, without seeking further permission from her solicitor.

'That may well be, but we need certain questions answered to help figure out who did,' Kennedy said, in a more conciliatory tone.

Suzi nodded and Chris re-asked the question.

'OK, which member of your support group reached out to Linda Joyce?'

'I believe it was Cecelia Harris.'

'Thank you,' Chris paused to let Suzi stew a bit in her discomfort at having to mention the other woman's name out loud.

'This group SASI, is it a privately funded operation?'

'Yes, we mostly work off donations and fundraising.'

'And you and Ms Harris are both members?'

'Volunteers actually, but yes.'

'Is this particular group aimed at male and female victims of sexual assault?'

'I'm not sure what difference that makes, but both.'

'How many male victims have availed of your services, would you say?'

'Detective, this line of questioning is making me very uncomfortable...'

'Sorry, just trying to establish some facts.'

'I wouldn't have exact numbers for that.'

'Maybe hazard a proportional guess. Fifty-fifty, eighty-twenty maybe?'

'You won't be surprised to hear it's primarily female, Detective. But that is very much by circumstance rather than design.'

'Ms Harris operates a social media account Forbidden Fruit, closely associated with this group and its members. What can you tell me about that?'

'You'll have to ask her, Detective, I know nothing about that side. My main function within the group is to help raise awareness and secure funding.'

'Very well, we will,' Chris said, suspecting she knew far more than she was letting on. 'Linda's brother, Ben. Do you know him personally?'

'Like I said, I got to know the whole family. During and after the trial, but especially after Linda's passing. That family was ripped apart by what happened, as was I.'

'I can only imagine, it was a terrible tragedy. They must have been devastated.'

'Yes they were.'

'You had become personally close with Linda?'

'Yes, I tried to support her and failed. Especially after that ... hashtag went viral. Her taking her own life hit us all hard.'

'Not least her brother, I'd imagine. The thought of what happened to his sister and not being able to protect her...' Kennedy said trailing off as he shook his head.

'Ben is one of the good guys. If you brought me here to ask if I thought he had anything to do with Will's death, I'd say very unlikely. He is a gentle soul.'

'Speaking of Vines, it seems you also knew him in a more personal capacity,' Chris said, checking her response carefully. 'To the point of been pictured together.'

But she didn't even flinch. 'It's a small town and the celeb world is even smaller, so we ran in the same circles. Will and I ... crossed paths at various events on any number of occasions. I never liked the guy, and when those accusations were made against him I liked him even less.'

'Yet you had no issue being pictured with him at such events - even after Linda's death?'

Suzi shrugged. 'Like I said, it's a small town. And he was found not guilty after all. What happened to Linda was a tragedy, but none of us could change that.'

Chris was taken aback by her blatant hypocrisy and again struck by how utterly desperate these online figures were to hold on to their self-proclaimed, trumped-up celebrity that they protected that status, no matter what. Almost to the point of being soulless.

It was depressing.

'Maybe, but you said yourself, what happened to Linda was tragic. And it hit everybody hard. Anger and guilt can be powerful stimulants - an eye for an eye and all that.'

Again he studied her as he purposely used the phrase, trying to see a flicker of reaction. The general public and media knew nothing of David Walsh's mutilation or the apples.

But her expression remained calm and unflinching.

'What about David Walsh?'

'What about him?' Suzi asked.

'It appears there was no shortage of bad blood between you two either. Especially after as you yourself mentioned, the unfortunate hashtag that was apparently the final humiliation for Linda Joyce.'

'Someone like David and I would've never seen eye to eye,' she muttered darkly and Chris tried not to read too much into her usage of the rather commonplace expression, but it was difficult not to. 'To me, he was the worst example of mankind, an apologist with no empathy for women and the challenges we face.'

'And what of Sean Shaughnessy?'

She sniffed. 'I saw him in action in the courtroom, the way he carried on smirking while Linda was being cross-examined. Shocking stuff indeed. Another man of no great loss to the world.'

'Suzi...' her solicitor warned, but Chris could tell that her disgust for all three men was primarily academic.

As much of a man-hater she professed to be, he didn't think she had it in her.

OUTSIDE THEY CONFERRED PRIVATELY for a bit. 'What do you reckon?' Kennedy asked.

'I think the only thing she's guilty of is being an attention-seeking shit-stirrer, though not enough to act on anything. I'm more interested in Harris, to be honest. Her anti-male sentiment is so extreme it could well be considered incitement.'

The two grabbed coffees from the nearby dispenser and headed in to meet their next interviewee.

Cecelia Harris - a heavyset woman dressed all in black - sat patiently with a neutral expression, her hands placed on the table in front of her, though she'd chosen not to bring along legal counsel.

She smiled as they greeted her in the manner of school-teacher smiling at a pupil; I'm friendly but don't mess with me.

The detectives set about questioning her - asking many of the same questions they had put to Suzi Cox and she reeled off answers in a matter of fact tone and without hesitation.

'I understand you're not married yourself ... are you in a relationship at the moment?' Kennedy asked, out of the blue.

'Well, Detective, that's a bit ... personal,' Harris replied, somewhat taken aback. 'I'm fortunate to be born asexual. Unbound by the weakness of desire.'

Chris could only imagine his partner's train of thought at this. Fluid, asexual ... all this modern-day categorisation was yet another a bone of contention for Kennedy who firmly believed life was black and white and grand as it was.

Whereas he himself tried to be more open minded.

'But you are a self proclaimed feminist, yes?'

Harris smiled and looked up at the ceiling before renewing eye contact. He was surprised by her unblinking ability to look straight at you, she was not a lady short of confidence.

'Yes, Detective, of course I'm pro women - I am one after all. To my mind, the word feminist has changed, it's no longer fit for purpose.'

'Your online mission statement and accompanying social media discourse - would you also describe this as pro women?'

'Absolutely.'

'Forbidden Fruit - does that relate to the known religious expression?'

She exhaled. 'No, as it happens. Detective, I'm also lucky to be a-religious.'

'Yet the accompanying imagery is clearly religious in nature. Eve in the garden of Eden with the apple?'

'I would class it as historical, so much as religious actually.'

'How so?'

'Because all traditional history; both fact and fiction, has been recounted by men. And almost always to the detriment of women. But my own orientation puts me in a unique situation. I do not have a dog in this fight.'

'I'm not sure I'm with you?' Chris said, puzzled.

'The battle of the sexes of course. Men have always resented women, it's their weakness, the desires they are born with, yet the ones they cannot act on. Legally anyway. In modern society however, there are those who can't resist those urges, hence the need for the services SASI provides. Throughout history, those that could resist, suffered consequences.'

Chris noticed that her demeanour had changed slightly now, considerably less relaxed and more ... impassioned.

'Consequences?' Kennedy prompted, urging her to explain further.

'Hate, blame, shame, there are many words to describe it. Do you truly believe that a naked couple was warned not to eat an apple from a tree, and that the woman seduced the man to do so? To me that sounds like blame. Wars have been fought and lost through history by men's uncontrollable desires. Women have always been the collateral damage, and still here we are. In an age where the highest courts in the land; its corridors paced by men in suits, still protect the victims of a man with no control over his urges.' She clasped her hands together. 'I just want women to stop apologising for a problem that isn't of their own making.'

'And what about justice?' Chris asked thinking of the emoji scales used as her single summation of the three men's recent demise.

'That is definitely not for any of us to decide.'

51

Back in the GFU lab, Reilly stood on the opposite side of the workstation to Lucy - a large sealed evidence bag on the table separating them. 'The colour does look about right.'

'Not just the colour. Texture and consistency too,' the younger tech said, holding a small transparent plastic sleeve which contained a single strand of hair. 'We just need to prove with one hundred percent accuracy that it's the same.'

Reilly pulled on some gloves and proceeded to spread out on the workstation the green hooded jacket that Lucy had brought back from Ben Joyce's apartment.

The edge of the hood was trimmed with synthetic fur; its inconsistent brownish-grey shading having caught Lucy's eye.

The jacket itself seemed old and well-worn, and the inside label read *Primark* - the popular Irish chain store, which unfortunately meant the garment wasn't especially unique.

'Let's run a couple of fibres through the spectrophotometer for starters.'

Lucy went to work rolling the jacket for debris, while Reilly viewed some of the synthetic fibres under the microscope.

When she'd finished. she filed and labeled a slide before preparing the wet-vac to use it on the jacket once Lucy had finished dry-rolling.

The two worked in tandem without much conversation. Until Lucy approached with a gleam in her eye and a small clear bag containing a strand of fair hair.

Actual human hair this time.

'Blond?'

'Longish too.'

'I was thinking the jacket seemed a little on the feminine side to be Joyce's.'

So who was the female? Reilly wondered. And was the owner of this jacket acting as Ben Joyce's accomplice, or his avenger?

HAVING SENT all info through to the detectives, the weed alone being enough to keep Joyce detained, Reilly caught up with Daniel again in the Westbury hotel restaurant.

'How did the lecture go?' she enquired, relating

to his guest appearance at Trinity, the apparent reason for his out of the blue visit.

'Really good, excellent panel actually - some brilliant speakers. You know me, I'm not really the guy for large presentations.'

She smiled inwardly, knowing that he was indeed the very guy for these presentations.

'How about you - sounds like a break in the case?' he asked, pouring her a welcome glass of red wine.

'Maybe.'

He regarded her thoughtfully. They'd already discussed the investigation in detail on the way back from the airport, Daniel as always, far more interested the killer's state of mind, than any victim's suffering.

'Yet you don't seem all that ... energised.'

Reilly sighed, deciding she might as well come clean. He could always read her like a book anyway. 'I am - it's just, I guess I'm not feeling as ... invested as usual.'

'In this particular case? Or the job in general?'

Man, he was always so maddeningly perceptive.

'The job in general. Maybe. I'm not sure. Everything just feels ... different lately.'

Daniel set his own glass down, and seemed to be choosing his next words carefully.

'What happened ... however you prefer to square it away, was still a monumental shock to the system, both physically and emotionally. I totally get you don't want to talk about this Reilly, especially given our shared involvement and I understand that, truly. But surely you realise that when you choose to actively dampen down an emotional response, it needs to vent itself somewhere, or somehow.'

She nodded. 'I know. But I'm just not ready... and I feel like I have no right anyway to ... grieve I suppose,' she admitted finally. 'It's no secret that I never wanted ... motherhood in the first place. Hell, I was in denial for months - it was Chris who figured it out long before I did.'

'Yes, Todd told me all about that. While I admit that initially I had great hopes for you two, in the end I feel you made the right decision. My son would not have been a good choice for you in the long run, much as it pains me to admit it.' He put a hand on hers. 'I know he wanted you to come back with him, and while you made no bones about the fact that your future isn't in Florida, are you still so sure that it remains here - in Dublin?'

She shook her head. 'I'm not really sure about anything, to be honest. Like I said, lately I'm getting the overall sense that my heart's no longer in it. And realising now that maybe I only came back that time because ...'

'Because of Delaney.'

She nodded, still afraid to admit it out loud.

'And how does he figure in all of this right now? I'm sure he understands that you're in a very difficult place emotionally.'

Chris understood all too well; that was part of the

problem.

'I haven't really been confiding in him recently, not since ... everything. I dunno ... lately I just feel like I'm going round in circles.'

'You mean you pushed him away.'

Reilly nodded. 'I just hate for him to see me as someone who always needs rescuing - like an injured puppy or something,' she admitted, her fists tight.

'Oh come on, that's the very last way anyone who knows you would choose to describe you. And from what I myself know of Delaney, it sounds like far from rescuing you, he's *supporting* you, like any good partner would. But you're actively spurning that.'

She exhaled. 'I was always great at pressing the self-destruct button.'

'That's not what happened here and you know it. From a medical point of view, these things are so often a complete mystery - and you and I can appreciate better than most that a neat resolution isn't always achievable.'

Doctor Moore had told her pretty much the same thing. 'Of course I know that, but I can't help thinking that ... that maybe I deserved it, or more that I didn't deserve to be happy.'

She hung her head, still ashamed by the painful truth she felt in her heart. And always would.

'Nonsense,' he insisted forcefully. 'Of course you deserve to be happy - which is exactly why I'm glad you told my son to take a hike.' He smiled. 'But you certainly can't blame yourself for this, and I wonder if perhaps you're feeling more and more adrift the longer you're away from home. Have you truly considered coming back, on your own terms I mean - to see your dad, catch a wave, have some fun, even? Even for just a vacation like the one you were supposed to take at my place that time.'

The idea of a vacation right then sounded incredible. As did the thought of spending some chilled-out time back home. Free from worry, denial.

And soul-crushing guilt.

'I don't know ... I'm not sure if I could even get the time off ...'

'Of course you could. You would've been taking a sustained leave period in any case, all things being equal,' he pointed out, referring to her maternity leave. 'If you of all people aren't feeling it on the job Reilly, then you're not being true to yourself. And godammnit, after everything you've been through, you need a break. Feels to me like this is the perfect time to shake things up. Only then can you truly decide where your heart - and future lies.'

Then he put a comforting hand on hers. 'And speaking of your heart ... I'd advise that you properly discuss all this with Delaney, who I'm sure will also have some bearing on your decision. Invite him along even.'

'Chris? The last thing he'd want to schlep all the way back to the US on vacation with me. He's got a job to do too.'

'Perhaps, but in any case, I think you two need to

sit down and have it out, properly.' Daniel urged, his tone brooking no nonsense. 'You said it yourself - you keep going round in circles. So whatever the hell's going on between you two; now is a good time to square this thing away once and for all.'

52

'Please tell us you have something else? Joyce's solicitor is all over us like a rash now,' Kennedy pleaded the next day.

'Well, good morning to you too,' Reilly chided.

'What about the jacket?'

'Joyce says he never saw it before. When we told him it was hanging up in his digs, he said it could be an old girlfriend's.'

'No flatmates, so it has to be,' Chris said, perching on the edge of her desk and handing Reilly a fresh coffee, which she gratefully accepted.

It had been a long night. And way too much to think about after her conversation with Daniel. Sleep was as always, collateral damage.

'Old girlfriend, he said?'

'Yes. He was seeing someone around the time Linda died, but they weren't going out that long.'

'Huh. Rory found this on his Facebook account.'

She handed him a printed image of Joyce with his arm around a blonde girl, alongside a harbour with fishing boats in the background. 'Check out the jacket.'

'*The* jacket?' Kennedy said, peering at the picture.

'Seems to be.'

'When we talked to the campus accommodation office, they had no record of anyone living there with him, so he must've moved her in on the sly,' Chris said. 'She's not registered at DCU or any other colleges in the city.'

'So you have a name then.'

Chris flicked through his notebook. 'Lia Mueller. Joyce said she was of German origin and that they weren't together all that long.'

'Well, that picture was taken six weeks ago.'

'There's something off here, all right,' Chris muttered. 'His phone records show no contact with this girl at all. And little to nothing on social media for her either - besides that photo.'

'I'd hazard this young one's about what eighteen, nineteen?' said Kennedy, looking again at the photo. 'Unless she has no phone, which basically makes her a unicorn.'

'I'll get Rory back on it.'

'Joyce also said he doesn't know where the ex is living now, so Sarah's running the name with social services and the health boards,' Chris said.

'What about Cox and Harris?' Reilly asked then. 'The whole forbidden fruit angle.'

He shook his head. 'Just militant feminist stuff especially Harris - I actually found her a little scary to be honest, but not a lot else.'

'That one's a right weapon,' Kennedy spat dismissively. 'I've spent my life teaching my girls that they're equal to anyone regardless of gender, and the other one's brand of feminism is pure poison. Trying to persuade young girls that they're better than men is just as damaging if you ask me,' he grunted, crossing his arms across his chest.

'Rory's still trawling through Harris's online footprint to see if some fan or follower didn't get overly inspired by her takes,' Reilly told him.

'Anything else from Joyce's digs besides the coat and cannabis?'

'Coming together slowly, but it's starting to look pretty damning. The mat in his place also had traces of that insect-flour substance we found on Walsh, and at Vines' place. Interestingly, Lucy also found a discarded bottle containing remnants of moonshine, or what was the Irish word again?'

'Poitín.'

'Yes, in the garbage. Similar to the stuff in Vines' apartment. Difference is, the bottle was actually labelled.'

'As in branded?' Kennedy queried, puzzled. 'That makes no sense.'

'Take a look.' Reilly led them to the conference room where the catalogued evidence was laid out and labelled, and retrieved the bottle in question before handing it to Kennedy.

'Bug-in juice...' He read the handwritten label. 'Not a poitín description that I've ever heard of. Would this stuff be made from spiders too?'

'You're half right - crickets actually. And it is eighty percent proof.'

'Bug-in ... could it be some kind of modern slang for hooch maybe?' Chris mused.

'Didn't ring a bell around here anyway,' Reilly said, at the same time as Kennedy's phone began to ring.

'Sarah,' he mumbled to them, connecting quickly. 'Hey, what's up Buttercup?' he greeted the other detective, and she had to smile at his penchant for nicknaming professional colleagues. While she didn't know Sarah all that well, she guessed that the younger woman had also learned to take the big man's quirks in her stride.

'Nice one ... thanks.' Hanging up, he nodded at Chris. 'Got a hit on the girlfriend, well the surname at least. Several GP visits by a family called Mueller in the Leinster region over the last couple of decades. Sarah's already spoken to some of the docs, two have no recollection, but another has said he distinctly remembers the family.'

'Great, did she maybe get a home address?'

'No, apparently they were crusties - used to come here on camping holidays from Germany the doc said,' and Reilly guessed he meant the family were hippy types. 'Once she had a lead on the name she was also able to track down library registration and a succession of visits over the years to different branches, again in the same vicinity.'

'Nice one.'

'Herself and Spud are heading down to interview the GP now, and she's sending us the library details - see if maybe we can find someone who knows anything more about this Mueller girl.'

Chris nodded. 'Great. In the meantime, we'll keep leaning on Ben Joyce since the evidence is mounting against him. If he's truly innocent in all of this and yet for some reason, won't give up the girlfriend ...' He went over to the bottle of alcohol on the table and re-read the handwritten label. 'It's funny ... I was only talking to Sarah about this whole insects as food thing yesterday. She says a friend of hers found out by accident they had an insect allergic reaction just recently.'

Kennedy made a face. 'Sarah's friend eats insects?'

'No, apparently most of us unknowingly consume them every day.'

Reilly smiled, figuring it out before Chris got a chance to finish. 'In coffee.'

'Yep,' He glanced at Kennedy, who with perfect timing, was taking a gulp of his Americano.

'What are you on about?'

She took up the mantle. 'Almost all commercial ground coffee contains a considerable amount of insect DNA. Cockroach DNA to be exact; it gets mixed up with the beans and then dumped into grinders at cafes.'

Kennedy looked at them both over the top of his cup before slowly lowering it. 'Cheers for that.'

'You want some Bug-in juice to wash it down?' Chris chuckled.

'Nah, you're grand thanks...'

Then Reilly thought of something. 'Bug in ... we're automatically thinking insects, right?'

The others nodded.

'Back home, bug in is a prepper term - to dig in and lay low if under attack.'

'I was thinking more of a sociable term - drink this and you'll be buggin or something ...' Kennedy ventured.

But the wheels were well and truly turning now.

'Ask whoever's working Ben Joyce to push him hard on where he got that stuff,' she said, her tone more urgent. 'I have a hunch and if I'm right, then everything we're seeing is finally starting to make some sense.'

53

Having arranged a fresh round of interrogation with Ben Joyce's solicitor for later, the detectives decided in the interim to chase down the library-related lead for his girlfriend, Lia Mueller.

'What did O'Brien say when you told him about Selena and the leak?' Chris asked, as having left the GFU building, they drove onto the ramp to join the motorway circling the capital. 'Did he blow a gasket?'

'Strangely OK actually, I was expecting a meltdown. There'll will be a review up the chain at some stage, but he's holding off on it all until this is sorted.'

'I'm sure it'll just be a slap on the wrist.'

'Hope so. Selena's in bits over it to be fair, fallen out with her so-called friend who passed it on, having sworn secrecy. Honest to God, some of these kids would sell their own grannies for likes and shares.'

'Hard to keep anything secret these days.'

As they started to clear the heavier traffic and began moving faster towards their destination to the west of the city, they sat in silence listening to the news on the radio.

Speaking of secrets ... D day on the new position was fast approaching, and Chris still couldn't understand why he was finding it so hard to bring the subject up.

Especially when he'd pretty much made up his mind about what he was going to do. He needed a change, pure and simple.

'I've a bit of news from HQ myself.'

'Oh?'

'They've offered me that Chief of Operations role that was going.'

'Ha, you a Park desk jockey - seriously?' Kennedy scoffed, glancing over at Chris before returning his eyes to the road. 'Feck, you are serious, sorry.'

He had to smile. 'Yeah.'

'When ... I mean, are you going for it?'

'Hard to decide really, it's a big decision,' he lied.

'Feck. That is a bit of news.'

'I didn't want to say anything until I knew more myself, but they've officially offered the position to me now.'

'So when would ... I mean, how much longer before - '

'I have to let them know by the end of the month and I'd imagine things'll move pretty fast then.'

'Christ, that's huge, bud. I don't know what to say. I mean obviously, you've to do what's right for you. But feck ...'

'What about yourself?'

'Me? 'Oul fellas like me don't like changes in routine.'

'You'd swear you were ready for the pension, sure you're only a young fella yet.'

'Not for this job. Anyway O'Brien might have me pushing pens soon too as penance, so could be all change around here anyway.'

'Nah, you'll be grand,' Chris assured him, as they approached the outskirts of the small West Dublin location in which the library was located. 'Anyway, as I said, I'm not sure what I'm going to say yet, but when I do, you'll be the first to know.'

'What about Steel?'

He flinched a little. 'What about her?'

'Well, I know she hasn't said much about that whole business ... in fairness, she hasn't said *anything*, but I know you were... well I know the two of ye are close, closer than me anyway, and obviously I wouldn't know what to say...'

'You know Reilly - seems to take everything in her stride.'

He nodded solemnly. 'Josie was the very same. Even after she still had to go through the whole delivery palaver knowing there'd be nothing at the end of it. A warrior, she was.'

Chris looked at him. 'Jesus Pete, I didn't realise ...'

'Ah that was years ago, before Selena - and long before I even knew you. But no joke all the same; I wasn't sure what was going on, or even which way was up for half of it; Josie took care of it all - including herself. I tell you, women are a hell of a lot stronger when it comes to these things, no doubt about it,' he said solemnly. 'Yer wan Cox and her cronies banging on trying to stir division ... honestly I don't think those women even realise what proper equality means.'

54

Emmy scurried through the gorse bushes as far as the pile of moss-covered rocks. Crawling around the back, she started to slide under the slender gap that led to the mouth of the tunnel.

She brushed away the layer of loose dirt mixed with leaves and old twigs, which looked like it hadn't been disturbed since she herself had used it to cover the trapdoor entrance last year.

Finding the finger hole, she placed her thumb, index and middle fingers into it and pulled the door up until it lifted enough for her to slide beneath and through to the yard.

She wasn't sure what she'd say when faced with her sister, who she knew would be furious and full of told-you-sos.

All those years of listening to what Mama had

taught them but she of course had known better, or at least she thought she did.

And when Mama died, she needed to find out for herself.

Securing the hatch, she reached above to a ledge beside it, feeling her way in the pitch darkness again and breathing a sigh of relief when her fingers found the small flashlight.

Pressing the on button she held the torch in one hand as she started to shimmy along the tunnel out to the yard behind the pig pen which she could already smell.

Once she'd negotiated a similar trapdoor at the other end and scrambled out, she moved towards the steel post holding up one corner of the shed.

Reaching up, and with the flashlight in her mouth, she untied the thin cord wrapped in a loose knot around the post and tugged it gently. The small bell it was attached to began to chime, and about thirty seconds later, she heard a door click.

Then stood there, looking into the darkness until she heard a voice whisper.

'Who is it?'

'It's me...' she whispered, relieved afresh that the protocol hadn't changed. She was never going to take a chance walking across the yard unannounced, given their alert system - and her sister's aim with a shotgun.

She moved swiftly across the space and threw her arms around her sibling, tears starting to flow.

'Oh Em, I was so worried,' Cici said, hugging her close. 'Are you OK?'

'Yes, you were right - I should never have left ... I'm sorry.'

'Shh, it's OK. You're home now, you're safe.'

'I'm not so sure about that, Cici,' she said, sniffing determinedly. 'We need to get ready. The day of reckoning has finally arrived.'

55

'Here we are - the place with the blue shopfront ...' Chris mumbled, pointing to a pair of large windows and double doors with the name 'Newcastle Library' written over the door.

Kennedy pulled into the small parking area beside the single-story pebble dashed building. Exiting the car, they walked into the reception area, where a librarian sat at a low desk facing a computer screen.

The library branch was small; with only five or six rows of bookshelves and a seating area with a couple of desks, seats and a few reading chairs. An elderly man sat on one of the softer armchairs, resting a hand on his walking stick while reading a book with the other.

He looked up as the detectives walked in and nodded by way of a greeting. He was unshaven with wrinkled clothing that made Chris suspect the musty smell in the room was not just emanating from the older books.

On the far side of the room was a mother reading to her child from a well handled pop-up picture book likely covered in every germ known to man.

'Hello,' he greeted, 'we're here to see Jackie?'

'Oh yes, she's out in the back office, I'll give her a shout. Take a seat.'

Chris and Kennedy thanked her and waited as the small toddler looked up from his book to stare suspiciously at the two of them.

'Not a bad day.' The older man said, sizing them up as they nodded in agreement. 'Ye local?'

'No, from the Big Smoke,' Chris replied pleasantly.

'Long way to come for books,' he said, smiling at his own joke.

Just then the door behind the reception desk opened and an older woman walked out, beckoning them to follow her into the rear office.

'Hello Detectives, How can I help you?' Jackie the senior librarian, said.

'You spoke to Detective Sarah Davis earlier about a member who was apparently a regular here some time ago. Lia Mueller?'

'Yes, I pulled out the file right after I spoke to your colleague,' the librarian confirmed, taking a couple of postcard sized cards from a box in front of her. 'All our more recent records are on computer these days,' she mumbled, putting on her reading glasses.

'What can you tell us about the girl?'

'Well, not a lot specifically, given she was named on a family membership. According to the records, the Muellers were prolific readers and the list of borrows is extensive, from our branch alone.'

'Is it possible for us to get a list of borrows and accompanying dates?'

'I'd have to check the old privacy rulebook first on that one,' Jackie demurred uncertainly.

'That's OK, we can save you the bother,' Kennedy slid an official Freedom of Information request across the table.

'Brilliant.' She read through it quickly and nodded.

'Would you remember the girl yourself?'

'I think I remember the family. Visitors to the area they said, at one of the campsites, I think. Mother was nice enough and the kids seemed shy.'

'Kids?'

'Yes, two girls, about three or four years between them I'd say.'

'Description?' Kennedy asked.

'Well, all blonde and with foreign accents - German maybe? The impression I got was that the dad came to Ireland to work as a contractor for two or three months at a time, and the family came to see him and now and again, in the summer mostly. It's only when I received the call earlier, that I realised they were using other libraries in the area too.'

'You said you got the impression, was that one you drew yourself or ...?'

'It's such a long time ago since they joined, but I do believe that's what the mother or maybe one of the girls said, hang on a moment...'

Jackie walked over to a filing cabinet and opened and closed a few drawers until she found what she was looking for.

'Here it is,' she said placing a folder on the table and opening it. 'This is their original membership application,' she added, scanning a document. 'They seem to have applied as non-residents, and you didn't need a whole lot by way of ID back then. Here we go - family membership under the lead name, Mueller.' She handed the document to Chris.

'Excellent thanks. Can you provide us a printed account of their borrow history too?'

'Of course, but just be aware the computerised system was brought in a few years after they joined, so that earlier period won't be covered.' Jackie tapped some keys on the PC keyboard that caused the printer to wake from its slumber and start to hum before it began to eject pages.

'This is some heavy reading,' Chris commented, as he flicked through the pages. There was a lot of encyclopaedia, historical and some animal husbandry-related stuff too, which was interesting.

'Seems to be mostly non-fiction,' he mumbled to the librarian, who nodded.

'I got the sense that they might be the home-schooling type if you know what I mean.'

'What was the last date you do have borrow activity recorded?' Kennedy asked, glancing at the date on the sheet.

'No borrows at all logged in the last few years anyway,' Jackie commented, scanning the system. 'Looks like they stopped reading altogether, or more likely just seduced by all the digital stuff.' She rolled her eyes. 'Seems like everyone is eventually.'

56

Later, back at the station they took another crack at Ben Joyce.

'OK, formalities out of the way first,' Chris told the solicitor. 'We're preparing the paperwork to formally press charges. One count resisting arrest, one count of failure to cooperate, as well as a couple of other misdemeanours - namely illegal alcohol and cannabis possession. And most important of all, withholding evidence.'

'And to be clear, this is just for starters while the investigation is ongoing,' Kennedy put in, leaving no room for the solicitor to interject. 'Ben, your parents are downstairs. I know they've already spoken to you, urged you to start helping us out before it's too late,' he said, leaning forward. 'One way or another we *will* find out what's going on. If that's with your help it will reflect better on you. If you keep refusing ... well I think Mr Hobbs here can outline the ramifications.'

'Detectives, we've had a discussion in the interim. My client is now willing to cooperate as long as certain assurances are given.'

'Go on ...'

'Mr Joyce's co-operation would be conditional upon the following,' He handed a document to Chris.

'This isn't Netflix, lads - you don't get to make demands,' Kennedy snorted while Chris read the sheet.

'I don't see anything too problematic here. Perhaps you'd like to start by telling us the truth about your friend Lia Mueller and her involvement in all of this?'

Ben looked away, his expression defeated.

REILLY'S PHONE vibrated on her hip as she reviewed the evidence with a fresh eye, taking into account her brainwave from before.

'Well?'

'It's definitely the girlfriend. Ben Joyce confessed everything - or all he knows at least. I'm emailing you now with a map of known locations the Mueller family frequented over the years. Maybe cross-reference that gleysol wetland terrain you mentioned in relation to the apple trees, or stuff from the shoe treads and all that.'

'On it,' she replied, opening the email attachment. 'You spoke with the library?'

'Yep. Seems the family gave the impression of being tourists. Ben Joyce confirmed that Lia, full name Emilia Mueller, has lived here all of her life.'

'Does he know where she is now?'

'Apparently not. Seems this is not the kind of family altogether welcoming to outside visitors ...'

Makes sense.

'Emilia and her sister were raised completely off-grid, no school, no social interaction outside of the family unit,' Chris continued. 'That label on the poitín? Nothing to do with insects or partying, it's exactly like you said - a prepper term. To bug in off-grid when the shit hits the fan in the outside world.'

Reilly exhaled. She was right.

'Evidently Emilia got tired of that life, and more curious about the outside world. Ben said he first met her while working a summer job at a hardware place when she came in with her sister to buy supplies. He said he found her a breath of fresh air, no interest in phones, internet or any modern conveniences. Reckons was more of a tomboy type - at one with the outdoors, and a dab hand at practical stuff. Almost like a female MacGyver he said.'

'What was she buying?' Reilly asked, her mind racing now. 'When he first met her at the hardware store.'

'Didn't think to ask to be honest. I will though. But here's where it gets even more interesting,' Chris continued. 'For someone who had no interest in modern life, she became hooked on social media in particular. Especially around the time of his sister's trial.'

So it was she, not Ben who was behind the interactions with Cox and Harris, Reilly realised. And the murders too.

The scales of justice.

'Apparently so,' Chris confirmed, when she raised the query. 'Exacting revenge on the men whose actions she believed responsible for Linda's death.'

'But why was Ben protecting her?' she asked, puzzled.

'He maintains she was adamant she was only acting on his behalf. All throughout the trial he'd been making throwaway remarks about the likes of Vines, and then once the hashtag thing kicked off, David Walsh too - hoping they died screaming and stuff. He didn't realise that Emilia took these things literally. An eye for an eye and all that. She was raised to view everything pragmatically. And it seems, to kill if needs be.'

'Why the hell didn't he go to the authorities? After Shaughnessy at least.'

'Says he honestly didn't suspect a thing, figured like us all at first, that it was probably just Shaughnessy's gangland associations. But then when Walsh went missing, he started to wonder.'

'And why he was hanging around Vines' place that time by the canal. When the news broke, he figured she was behind that too?'

'Yes. Then afterwards, having scarpered on the

bike, he went home and had it out with her; they had a huge argument and he said he was ... afraid.'

'Afraid of the girlfriend? I don't blame him.'

'So he promised he'd cover for her, but in the meantime she should go home and lay low until everything blew over.'

'Back to where she was raised?'

'Yes. Joyce says he doesn't know the exact location, but she mentioned their 'farm' to him from time to time. Taken with his recollections, plus the GP and library information, we can put together a general location. But with the soil profile and satellite mapping in the area, we should be able to narrow it down a lot more.'

'I'm on it.'

Still, it would be one thing to find the location, Reilly thought grimly; but if this truly was a prepper compound, quite another to infiltrate.

57

'We've overlaid the soil and rock profile map to the co-ordinates, and we're looking at a radius of about twenty miles plus,' Reilly said, laying out the large scale map for the detectives to examine a few hours later.

'But based on the limited information Joyce provided, we also know we're looking for an area with some key features,' Chris pointed out. 'A house or farm building with outbuildings and a courtyard. According to him, Emilia mentioned feeding animals in the paddock, so some open fields in close proximity too.'

'No shortage of farm buildings in that neck of the woods, that's all you'll find out that way,' Kennedy said, surveying the map - a largely rural area, west of the city. 'Any other prominent features we need to know about - there must be something. An orchard ... the apples?'

'And if they were self sufficient, polly-tunnels maybe,' Chris mused.

'Polly-tunnels?' Reilly enquired.

'Those tunnel shaped garden structures you sometimes see, with sheets of polythene stretched over semi circle bars and closed off at both ends. Acts like a greenhouse, and mostly used to grow vegetables and protect them from the climate.'

'Handy to spot on satellite imagery too,' Kennedy said, sitting down at his desk with a coffee, and bringing up a mapping site.

The area in question was indeed scattered with a mix of farm buildings, and some of the satellite imagery was poor, as was often the case with more remote countryside areas.

'Anything?' Chris asked impatiently, his gaze continuing to scan while he manipulated the screen cursor with the mouse.

'Possibly,' Reilly mumbled. 'Here's a place that looks like it could have those tunnels you mentioned, but there's a car park adjoining, so it seems to be just a garden centre maybe. Then this ...' She zoomed in on what looked to be a sparsely populated area of hillside adjacent to a minor country road - like an agricultural laneway. 'See those farm buildings, a courtyard and ... could that be a greenhouse?'

'Can you zoom in a bit more?' Chris urged, indicating the laneway. 'There. It looks like stone pillars and a gate closest to the lane.'

Kennedy squinted and shrugged. 'No shit Sherlock.'

'But then ... so does this,' he continued, pointing to where another laneway just up from the gates wound its way through vegetation before coming to what looked like a second set of gates. 'The boundary seems to extend all the way down to this river or stream or whatever, along the bank and around to circle this whole area. Zoom out a bit now.'

'This outside boundary seems to be walled also?' Reilly pointed to a greyish border on the map.

'A lot of land around those parts would have once been part of larger estates owned by wealthy families. You can often tell by the old stone walls and groups of smaller cottages nearby formerly used to house people who worked the estates,' Chris mumbled, peering over her other shoulder.

'That second gate seems to be part of this inner boundary. And this area in between looks pretty overgrown with thick vegetation.'

'Why would anybody need two sets of gates?' Kennedy asked.

Chris shrugged. 'Maybe another set to keep animals in - like a livestock pen? Hard to tell from an arial shot.'

Reilly bit her lip. 'Or to keep the rest of the world out.'

58

Cici had the laptop open, watching in rising panic at the flickering live security footage of a couple of cars and four men - two in uniform - wandering around in front of the outer gates.

'Who did you tell?' she urged her sister angrily.

'Nobody, I told nobody, not even Ben, I swear.'

'Well, they've been hanging around for a while and it doesn't look like they're going away any time soon. We have to think of something.'

Emmy scowled. 'Just ignore them, they can't get near us unless we let them.'

'I'm wasn't going to let them in, I'm trying to think of a way to get rid of them.'

'It's my fault, they're here for me - I brought them here. It's all over.'

'Hey, we've spent our lives preparing for a day

like this - you don't throw yourself to the wolves as soon as they arrive at your door.'

'How did they even know how to find us anyway?' Emmy raged. 'I didn't tell Ben anything about this place. Oh, I can't believe I've been so careless.'

'You did what you thought was right. Tried to defend someone you loved. Just like Mama.'

Though she and her sister had always interpreted their mother's teachings very differently.

Cici believed educating and saving women from being wronged by men was far more preferable than avenging for it after the fact, like Emmy did.

An eye for an eye ...

And ultimately, Mama had done both.

'Let me handle it. I'll tell them they need to leave, and we will do now what we always planned - like she taught us.'

'Are we really ready though?' Emmy bit her lip. 'So much has changed since Mama passed. No, I've lived among them, let me. I can try and talk to them first and then if they don't go away ...' She glanced at the shotgun by the door.

'I think you've already done enough,' her sister said, her mouth set in a firm line. 'And I'm the one who's better at talking ...'

Thinking hard about what she was going to say, Cici zoomed in on the unwelcome visitors onscreen and catching sight of a face, drew a sharp intake of breath.

'Actually, it's too late for that now,' she told Emmy solemnly. 'Seems we've both been careless ...'

59

The detectives and local police stood surveying the outer gates, looking for a way around or through. There was no buzzer or keypad. The gates themselves were about eight foot tall and made of steel, with the tips of each bar sharpened to a point to make scaling them difficult.

There were weeds growing on the ground beneath and the remnants of old leaves and twigs blown up against the rails, indicating the entrance was not utilised very often.

'What do you reckon?' Kennedy asked, as the two locals pulled at the gates and reached through the bars to see if the electric motor could be disengaged.

'If that camera's working I think somebody already knows we're here,' Chris said, not liking the setup. If what Reilly had told them about prepper culture was even half true, this place was a fortress.

'How long till the warrant?'

'Spud's on it as we speak. But I don't think anybody's leaving here anytime soon.'

'True. But maybe we don't need a warrant if we suspect there are drugs present, with evidence possibly being destroyed while we stand here kicking our heels?' Chris pointed out archly.

'Huh?'

The weed Joyce had at his place. Who's to say there isn't a huge cannabis farm up there?'

'Nice one,' Kennedy smiled, liking this angle.

Chris approached the elder of the local cops. 'Where's the nearest fire station?'

'Down the town. About ten minutes away.'

'Any chance you'd give them the nod and get them up here ... discreetly?'

The officer duly made a few calls, and some fifteen minutes later, a small jeep emblazoned with fire service signage drove up, and a couple of lads jumped out.

After a brief chat, the two firemen went to work on the gates with the Jaws of Life machinery typically used to pry people from crushed cars.

'Better feckin' hope this is the right place, or the cost of that gate is going out of our wages,' Kennedy muttered, as he followed Chris and the others up along the laneway.

Just as they turned a corner further up, they spotted someone standing on the lane watching, as if transfixed. Then without warning, the heavyset woman turned and hurried off in the opposite direction once again out of sight.

Chris's eyes widened. *Was that ...?*

He paused, momentarily confused, while the others broke into a jog; the younger and faster of the two locals taking off ahead.

Chris was a few feet behind, the gap growing with every stride as Kennedy and the older detective took up the rear.

What was she doing here? Was she somehow involved with the Mueller family too?

Moments later, they heard shouting, and as Chris rounded the corner he could see the inner gates about to close - while the woman he was almost certain was Cecelia Harris and another, more sprightly female, hurried toward some outbuildings in the distance.

The first officer reached the gates seconds too late, as a screeching sound of metal on metal signalled their movement. Frustrated, he reached out to prevent their closure, and as he did Chris could only watch in horror as the guy's knees buckled at making contact with the metal, his body shaking violently.

With a few faster strides, he bridged the distance, but could already smell putrid burning flesh.

Resisting the urge to grab hold of the younger officer, he looked around the area and quickly fetched an old branch amid the hedgerow, shoving it between the guy's arms, hooking and pulling him backwards while being careful not to make contact.

He wrenched hard until the other man's grip was broken and the two flew backwards in a heap, the poor officer's dead weight pinning Chris down.

They were swiftly joined by the others as the guy's colleague frantically checked for signs of life, while a breathless Chris indicated for Kennedy to get help.

He sat up dazed, staring at the ramshackle house and building beyond, and got to his feet as the firemen swiftly appeared with a first aid kit and defibrillator, breathing heavily as they went to work trying to resuscitate the younger cop.

If suspicion of drugs was enough to go inside the perimeter initially, the booby-trapped gate and subsequent injury of a police officer was ample cause for a full on invasion.

As the ambulance sped away down the country lane, other tactical and support vehicles were called in.

'O'Brien's agreed to send down the rangers to clear the place,' Kennedy said, pacing.

The rangers were a trained Garda counter terrorism unit best suited to the situation. Even though Chris suspected they'd never been engaged to gain entry to a residential home and family before.

'Did you get a good look at yer wan?' the big man asked.

'Yes. I'm almost certain it was Cecelia Harris.'

'That one? Hardly Joyce's girlfriend surely?'

'Doubt it. The sister, maybe. Remember the librarian said there was a few years between them?'

'Damn. I knew Harris was suspect, all that weird highfalutin' talk out of her.'

With darkness falling and the arrival of the rangers imminent, Chris was unsure how this was going to play out, especially when by all accounts, these ladies seemed pretty au fait with what to do in a crisis situation.

'You think the whole Mueller family might be in there?'

'We have to assume so. I was a way back when I saw Harris at the corner and then got distracted by what happened at the gate, so I couldn't be sure how many people there were.'

Kennedy looked up towards the house. 'Looks quiet up there now, no movement. Hopefully the rangers'll prevent anybody squeezing through the perimeter.'

'This whole place seems fairly well-suited to keeping people out - can't imagine going the opposite direction would be any easier,' Chris said, the image of the poor officer's face as he was electrocuted etched into his brain, echoing Sean's Shaughnessy horrific cause of death.

This family obviously had form.

60

Darkness had fallen by the time the ranger unit arrived and set up base at the external gate.

Once the evening light had faded, no lights appeared inside any of the buildings. The only sound was that of livestock echoing inside the courtyard and throughout the fields beyond.

In the interim, the same fire officers had removed the gate and detached the security camera.

Kennedy quickly briefed the arriving unit's head of operations, and it was eventually decided to wait till daybreak the following morning to help the team get the lay of the land.

Kennedy called Josie to tell her he wouldn't be home for his lasagne, while Chris touched base with Reilly to put the GFU on alert to come at first light.

Hours later, the sky began to change to an inky blue and the horizon to the east started to brighten, while rangers in full body armour were briefed with the help of drone photography taken above the compound the evening before.

As per protocol, the command unit also made several attempts to hail the occupants. But had little expectations of a reply.

Chris and Kennedy took up a position where they could see the gates and the house beyond, which was still in complete darkness.

They watched as the rangers lined up behind a tactical vehicle with heavy bull bars on the front to be used to ram the second-gate entryway.

As they approached, the driver increased the speed slightly to gain momentum before making first contact, and the gates peeled open as the van passed through with ease.

Those on foot waited a little until the van had cleared so as to ensure there wasn't some other kind of booby-trap surprise.

The others picked up the pace to fall in closer to the van again, while a couple of rangers rounded each gate to find and disconnect the power source. The group continued creeping towards the house until about fifty yards from the cluster of buildings, where they fanned out to assume their assigned positions.

The detectives looked on through the emerging light, trying to make out any unexpected movement, as building by building, the team worked their way through the homestead; the distressed squeals of animals still the only audible sign of life.

Then after what felt like an eternity, they heard two loud bangs; followed by two further, louder explosions accompanied by flashes, signalling entry into the main house.

Some forty minutes later a second vehicle appeared and a ranger from the support van approached the detectives.

'Any sign?' Kennedy asked.

'House is clear, just doing sweeps of the outbuildings, but nothing as yet.'

'No sign of life at all?' Chris asked. 'What about the women we saw? Could they have escaped?'

'Not likely. We had the place covered. We'll be able to let you up in a bit,' the ranger assured them, as he answered some incomprehensible message on the radio strapped to his chest.

'Feck it. They must have sneaked out during the night,' Kennedy muttered, deflated.

'Don't see how, there's at least twenty-five bodies posted around the perimeter.'

'Obviously they know the lay of the land better than we do.'

'Well they would've had to have gone cross-country, and they'd have been spotted on the road.'

'Need to get the chopper in maybe. Set up roadblocks too.'

The two detectives went into overdrive, making arrangements for a manhunt to track down the

Mueller family, as the first full rays of sunlight broke through the trees.

'Detectives,' the ranger called out a little later. 'We have a problem.'

Following him inside the courtyard, they stopped by the stinking pig-pen as the squealing animals mistook them for people bearing breakfast.

'Here.' The ranger came to a stop where three others were gathered round a dark manhole opening in the ground.

Kennedy shook his head at Chris. 'Told you. How deep is it?' he asked.

Chris looked around. Lots of footprints in the immediate area, and he could see the steel loops protruding from the tunnel walls acting as footholds were slick with mud.

'About eight foot, leads off under the buildings towards the tree-line over there. We could only check the first couple of foot with a camera but have a couple of lads down there now.'

'Let's check out the house,' Chris suggested, as they headed across the yard.

Walking inside the ramshackle building was like stepping back in time. There was a strong smell of burnt peat and wood from the range. The walls were lined with shelves of jar containers filled with what looked like pickles and jams. and various books and newspapers were scattered all across the threadbare furniture.

It put Chris in mind of one of those TV hoarder programmes, and he was half-expecting a rake of dirty cats to be crawling around too. But the place appeared completely devoid of occupants, feline or otherwise.

One of the rangers was standing by a door that led off the kitchen.

'What's in there?'

'I'm not sure how to best describe it,' he said, standing to one side to allow them through. 'Larder I suppose.'

'Holy feck ...' Kennedy exclaimed, as he took in the adjoining room about thirty foot long.

'It's like a warehouse,' Chris picked up one of hundreds, if not thousands of food cans resting on floor-to-ceiling shelves on either wall, a narrow walkway down the middle. Every type of dried and tinned non-perishable food imaginable and enough water to last a very long time. Or was it water at all, he wondered, peering at the handwritten label.

'There's enough here to feed a feckin' army.'

'Or a family of four for a very long time ...'

'That's not the half of it - check out the basement,' the ranger said, pointing to a door at the other end of the space.

They walked through the corridor and started to descend the stairs as warm, musty smelling air rose to meet them.

Chris led the way shining his torch, as the sound of the rudimentary steps creaking was drowned out by a louder clicking noise that seemed to swirl around a large subterranean space beneath the dwelling.

'What the fuck is this?' Kennedy asked, shining his own torch around the space.

'Crickets ...'

The two stood in silence taking in the room, their torchlight invoking a louder response from the wall to wall insect colony.

There must have been thousands upon thousands of them housed live in large plastic barrels and covered in mylar insulation sheeting; the very same mylar, Chris suspected, used to 'roast' Will Vines.

They made their way back upstairs through the larder and out to the kitchen area, to find the ranger they'd just spoken to now groaning on the floor alongside a fresh pool of vomit.

'What the...?'

'Must have a thing about spiders,' Kennedy muttered. 'I'll get some help.' He moved to the door and called out to a group of rangers standing beside the tactical vehicle. 'Hey, one of your lads has just keeled over in here.'

One ranger reached for his radio, while another followed him back inside to where Chris was loosening the clothes around his neck.

'That's Shay, where's Doug?'

'Haven't seen anybody else. We've only been in as

far as here though,' he told them, as the other guy moved further into the house.

Barely moments later they heard him shout into his radio. 'Ranger down here too.'

Chris got to his feet and as he did so, the room began to spin, until seconds later he was on the floor beside the first ranger.

'Gas!' Kennedy shouted, dragging Chris through the doorway and outside, as he himself began to feel nauseous.

'Everybody move back, we need to clear this area - now!' The ranger commanded.

As the medics tended to the men with oxygen masks, the GFU van rolled up. Chris sat up disorientated, breathing deeply into the mask as he watched Reilly step out.

'I knew the air in there was weird, what do you think it is?' Kennedy asked the commander.

'That's not my immediate concern - the other end of that tunnel was locked from the inside and is impenetrable. We have to assume the suspects are still on the property somewhere.'

A fresh perimeter was set up as Reilly headed over to join them, looking concerned.

'You OK?' she asked, as Chris took a deep drink from a bottle of water.

'Grand, just a bit spaced.'

'What I don't understand is why they didn't use the underground tunnel to escape when they had the chance?' Kennedy was saying.

'Because they've bugged in,' Reilly said, her mouth in a firm line. 'Everything around here is carefully set up to prevent intrusion. Between the electrified gates and the gas, who knows what other surprises are in store...'

61

Some twenty minutes later, a couple of other rangers, this time in chemical suits, reappeared from the house and pulled back their head gear to talk to the commanding officer.

'Looks like the gas didn't just do a job on us,' the commander said grimly, rejoining the detectives.

'How so?'

'Our team has located another hidden door beneath the stairs leading into a second section of basement about the same size as the insect farm, or whatever that is.'

'What's in there?'

'The family,' Reilly replied, before the commander could. 'All dead?'

He nodded. 'Well, the women anyway - no sign of any male as yet, so we need to keep searching before we can declare the all clear.'

Once again they could only stand and watch as

the flurry of ranger activity continued around the house and outbuildings.

Then a while later the commander returned. 'We've located the parents.'

He motioned for them to follow as he walked along the side of the house.

'Our guys are just finishing up. All yours in ten,' he called back over his shoulder as he led them off the pathway towards a group of trees, some thirty meters or so from the house, and pointed at a small white cross set amongst the wildflowers.

'As you can see, the male has been deceased for some time. The mother, much more recent I would think.' He indicated the rectangle adjoining the older grave, which looked a lot more recent - a year to eighteen months maybe.

Chris peered at the cross, trying to make out the handwritten scrawl. 'Papa ...'

'Two thousand and one - or is it seven?' Kennedy squinted at the date. 'He's been dead awhile all right.'

'Want to order an exhumation?' the commander asked.

'No, this is a crime scene and that definitely isn't an official burial site,' Chris said, wondering if the family matriarch's more recent passing had triggered the daughters' decision to venture out into the outside world.

'There's something else you should see ...'

The commander headed back towards the house

before stopping beside a waist-high wall with a bulging dome-shaped rubber sheet over it.

'What's that?'

'I believe it's the gas source that terminated the occupants, and made yourself and my men pass out.'

They walked around it, looking at the steel edging and straps holding the rubber in place and making the tank airtight. 'Pretty elaborate booby trap.'

'I don't think it was a booby trap, Detective. Looks to be using human and animal waste to produce natural gas. That line goes to the kitchen,' The commander pointed to the pipe running toward the house. 'The pipe branching off leads to an outlet in the basement.'

'What's on the other end then? A cooking hob?'

'In the kitchen yes. In the basement, it's just a ballcock.'

AS THE GFU worked the scene for what was now more likely to be an inquest rather than a criminal trial, Reilly stood in the basement area where sisters Cecelia and Emilia Mueller lay huddled together in repose.

Their faces looked serene; the two embracing one another protectively for the very last time.

While she was familiar with US prepper culture, and knew of lots of folks back home who'd decided to go off grid preparing for nuclear war, global disasters, alien invasion ... you name it, she knew that it was uncommon for this country.

But while their parents had obviously taught them well, it seemed there had been a fatal flaw in the sister's preparations, one that they'd discovered only when it was far too late.

When opening the gas line to dispatch any intruders, they'd neglected to cut the supply to their hidey-hole, set up to bug in for as long as required.

And the poisonous gas flooding the basement that was supposed to have been the Mueller's fail-safe, had ultimately signalled their death knell.

62

'We're joined in studio today by Suzi Cox to talk about her new podcast, The Unfairer Sex. Suzi, you are most welcome back to the show...'

'Thank you, Tom.'

'OK, let's dive straight in. Two months on from the Mueller murders and subsequent death of the chief suspect and her sister, who it seems also happened to be a friend of yours...'

'Hardly a friend. I knew Cecelia primarily via social media and our mutual involvement in the support group. I wasn't to know she was using her mother's maiden name.'

'Indeed. In any case, the picture that has emerged on the topic and discussed at length on your podcast, seems to be one of gender-motivated justice. When did the battle of the sexes turn into open warfare?'

'I feel 'twas ever thus Tom; maybe just not from your

perspective. What I found most interesting in the aftermath of Emilia Mueller's actions, was a lot of nervous chatter from men. That awareness of perpetual danger and risk is something women feel all the time. For us it's inbuilt. Whether it be walking alone in the street, or going for a run, it's simply something all women learn to live with. Knowing what was possible after Emilia ... I think a lot of men got a tiny glimpse into that ever-permanent fear.'

'But Suzi, you condoned Emilia Mueller's actions at the time, and faced a huge backlash online and indeed from the police. Do you regret your stance now?'

'I never condoned what happened to any of those men. I simply poised the question; should misogyny itself not be treated with more contempt in our society? Much like racism has become unacceptable to the point that somebody can be arrested for it.'

'You yourself have been accused of feminist radicalisation by way of your social commentary - would you agree with that assessment?'

'Firstly Tom, I agreed to come on this show to talk about my podcast. Secondly, investigations are still ongoing, so I'm obviously going to keep my counsel in that regard. I will say one thing, though - everything I write and talk about, albeit on The Unfairer Sex or via my columns, is entirely factual. Some of it historical with regard to women's rights, other parts social commentary on how things have changed, not always for the better. And I am just so very tired of men ...'

. . .

'CAN YOU BELIEVE THIS SHITE?' Kennedy pressed the off button on the car radio. 'Yer woman is all over the place these days - on The Late Late Show tonight too supposedly. Tired my arse. She's feckin' *loving* this.'

'Finally her moment to shine. The Unfairer Sex - worth a listen, do you think?' Chris asked over his shoulder to Reilly who was in the back seat.

'Yeah, you're a woman. What do you think?' Kennedy chimed.

She chuckled. 'Thanks for the acknowledgment. Perhaps there's some truth hidden in what she says, but for the most part, I think Suzi Cox just loves the sound of her own voice.'

'Do you know - over the last while I've been wondering if maybe the Muellers weren't dead right altogether shutting themselves away from it all, the whole kit n' caboodle. The world surely has gone to hell in a hand-basket, when self-promoting shit-stirrers have more sway over people than common sense. Gender wars, me arse.'

Chris threw another conspiratorial grin back at her, as the three took a turn off the motorway that led to the airport.

Whereupon she was catching a flight home to San Francisco.

Having waited until the Mueller murder investigation and related evidence was fully wrapped, she had formally requested a leave of absence which O'Brien had granted, confident the GFU was in good shape and great hands in her stead.

Only Chris knew that she wouldn't be coming back.

While she'd been thorough and incisive as always throughout the latest investigation, she'd eventually confided in him, as she'd confessed to Daniel, that her heart was no longer in it.

And relieved to find that he was, as always eager to support her all the way.

Kennedy was still chattering away as they drove, and she figured it was his way of trying to stave off his discomfort about having to say goodbye.

'Dunno about you but I *never* viewed a woman as any different or lesser than me. Sure, aren't I married to one, have two teenage daughters - *and* a mother of course. Like all men.'

Reilly chuckled. 'If every man was like you, all would be right with the world.'

63

Eventually, Kennedy pulled in to the airport departures set-down area and stopped the car at the kerb, before getting out to help with the luggage.

Suddenly overcome with affection for the errant detective, Reilly stepped up and hugged him.

'I'm gonna miss you, Pete. Take care of Josie and the girls.'

His face reddening at this unexpected display of emotion, he embraced her back; perhaps conscious too that it could be some time, if ever, they had the opportunity to see one another again.

She was more than ready to close the book on her time in Dublin now, eager to move on to the next chapter.

Snagging a nearby luggage cart, Chris joined in transferring cases from the boot of the car, and then paused nervously alongside her - as if equally unsure what to do or say.

Until finally, he too stepped forward for an embrace.

'I'm going to miss your ugly face, you know,' he murmured.

'Ha, you'll be too busy off sunning yourself in California to miss the likes of me.'

'I'm serious. Look after this dirty ole' town, OK? And mind yourself.'

This time, Kennedy was unable to contain his emotions as he clapped his trusty partner of seven years on the back. 'Look after yourselves too, the pair of you.'

And then stood alone as Chris grabbed the luggage cart, and he and Reilly disappeared hand-in-hand into the airport terminal.

It seemed they'd both been at an impasse this last while; equally jaded of going round in circles and ready at last to take the next step.

What happened now was anyone's guess, but it didn't matter.

New adventures beckoned; and whatever next was on the horizon, Reilly was certain that she and Chris would, as always, figure it out together.

ABOUT THE AUTHOR

Casey Hill is the pseudonym of husband and wife writing team, Kevin and Melissa Hill. They live in County Wicklow, Ireland.

Translation rights to the USA Today bestselling CSI Reilly Steel series have been sold in multiple languages including Russian, Turkish, Japanese and more.

Enter the link into your browser to join the mailing list and be notified of future Casey Hill releases: http://eepurl.com/FFE2D

Connect with the author via social media below.

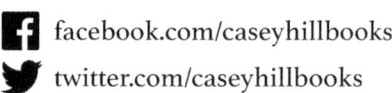 facebook.com/caseyhillbooks
twitter.com/caseyhillbooks

ALSO BY CASEY HILL

SERIAL

VICTIM

HIDDEN

THE WATCHED

QUANTICO

ONE LITTLE MISTAKE

PRETTY GUILTY SECRETS

THE PERFECT LIE

LAST GIRL ALIVE

Printed in Great Britain
by Amazon